Kieran Devaney was born in Birmingham in 1983. He now lives in Brighton. He is writing his second novel about a dog of infinite size. Find him at theapesofgod.blogspot.com, recollectionsofthegoldentriangle.tumblr.com, and davidcameron.tumblr.com.

DEAF AT SPIRAL PARK

DEAF AT
SPIRAL PARK

KIERAN
DEVANEY

SALT

CROMER

PUBLISHED BY SALT
South Lodge, Hall Road, Cromer NR27 9JG United Kingdom

© Kieran Devaney, 2013

First published by Salt Publishing, 2013

Printed in Great Britain by Clays Ltd, St Ives plc

Typeset in Paperback 9.5/14.5

ISBN 978 1 97773 16 7 paperback

1 3 5 7 9 8 6 4 2

For Rebecca

DEAF AT SPIRAL PARK

There was a bear. Life in the woods, where he lived with the other bears, had begun to sicken him.

The bear would go to the edge of the forest and watch the people who lived in the small town below. The stature of the buildings, the play of light on glass, the swish of fabric on pink, hairless flesh: these all moved this bear and he began to yearn. This was a bear that yearned.

On a cool night, this bear leaves the woods and enters the town. He breaks into a barber's and uses an electric shaver to remove all his fur, leaving just a small clump on the top of his head. The bear then breaks into a hardware store and, with a file, pares his claws until they are flat and dull. Finally, this bear steals the biggest shirt and pair of jeans he can find and strains them over his massive frame. On this night, looking at his reflection in the flat black glass of a shop window he begins to feel better. It is in this way that this bear becomes a man.

While working, the Recruitment Consultant called Carol usually had several windows open on her computer. Though the agency she worked for forbade their temps from using the internet wherever they were sent, she used it constantly. She loved, in particular, social networking sites. She maintained profiles on any number of them, detailing her favourite films, bands, books, TV shows, clothes, what character out of any character in the Harry Potter sequence of books she was, what character out of any character in the *Peanuts* series of books she was, what character out of any character she was out of the original line-up of the band Funkadelic, what character out of any character she was out of the TV series *Roots*, what artist out of any artist she was out of the Swiss Aktionist movement of artists, what early house track out of any early house track she was out of a list of early house tracks determined by her predilection for a certain bass sound over another bass sound. The profiles similarly accumulated digital camera photographs featuring the Recruitment Consultant, or parts of the Recruitment Consultant's body in various positions and locales. She always had her email open, both her work account and a personal account. She constantly had open the homepage of a tabloid newspaper and throughout the day she would click on stories and opinion pieces and by reading them she would learn a little something about the world.

✦

But the Recruitment Consultant didn't spend all her time on gossip websites and tabloid editorials. No. At least some of her time was taken up with putting people in jobs. And not just that! There was the whole business of interviewing people to see what kind of work they were suitable for, not to mention liaising with companies to see what kind of people they wanted to have working for them and what things they wanted those people to do.

Once she had a job to fill, this Recruitment Consultant had to think about all the people she had interviewed and decide which of them best suited the role that was available. This involved all kinds of sophisticated techniques such as trying to remember whether it was a particular English Literature graduate or a recent graduate of a Masters programme in French that had the more powerful forearms best suited to stacking a shelf. Or: out of a particular history graduate or a physics graduate, which has the most relevant skills for the job of putting the pieces of paper into alphanumerical order? Not just alphabetical order – that would clearly be the domain of the history graduate. Not just numerical order, which clearly suggests the physics graduate's particular skillset. But alphanumerical! Oh, it's a tricky one, combining as it does two potentially contradictory skills. If she sent the history guy, sure, he might be a whizz on the alpha side of things, the alpha side of things might not tax him one jot, but he could easily be an utter klutz in the numerical sphere. Then she'd be for it! Similarly, sending the physics graduate, you can sleep easy at night when considering the numerical side of putting the pieces of paper into alphanumerical order, but that alpha side is a rogue element. Who knows what might happen with it. This physics guy might ring her up from the job and probably say, Hi, Carol, how's it going? (. . .) Good, Good, (. . .) Well I'm OK, I guess I have good news and some bad news about the job. On the numerical side – this is the good news, by the way – I'm fine, I'm good. I've got the bits of paper in front of me and the numerical zone as regards them I've got entirely covered. It's no problem. That's the good news. But this . . . this alpha side, it's just not my thing, I'm out of my comfort zone with it, I don't mind telling you. If it was just the numerical I would be fine. But the whole alpha side of things, not to mention the combining the alpha with the numerical, has just left me stumped. It would probably be the same except in reverse if you got some guy in who was really good at the alpha side of the putting the pieces of paper into order. You know, that was really his thing. He loved it. That guy would probably call you up and say, Hi, Carol, how are you? (. . .) I'm fine thanks, but I'm having a bit of trouble with the numerical side of the putting the pieces of paper into order, into alphanumerical order. The alpha side is going great – I'm having a great time with it, I could do it all the livelong day. But this numerical side is awful tricky. I'm having an absolute dog of a time with it. I just don't get the thing. That's what someone good at the alpha but not at the numerical aspect might say to you, Carol, about the whole thing of putting the pieces of paper in alphanumerical order. Now

4

me, I'm just the opposite, funnily enough. With me the numerical stuff happens to be my particular forte, whereas my weakness – what lets me down in this type of situation – is the alpha side of the task. That's what I'm telephoning you about now. And the Recruitment Consultant would be the one who had to pick up the pieces. If the company had asked for two people to sort the pieces of paper into alphanumerical order then she could have sent both the history graduate and the physics graduate and they could have worked together. The history graduate could do the alpha and then pass the piece of paper onto the physics graduate who could do the numerical. Both had in the interviews expressed their fondness for working in teams. That arrangement would work out well. It would be effective. But the company had only asked for one person and so the Recruitment Consultant had to choose. She had no one on her books with both a physics and a history degree so she would have to decide between the two. The question was, when sorting the pieces of paper into alphanumerical order, which is the most important factor? Is it the alpha or is it the numerical? She could call up the company and talk to a manager there who would probably say, Hi, Carol, what you saying? (. . .) Yes, yes, I'm good too, thanks, (. . .) I do agree, that particular actor's career has certainly hit a downturn since he left that popular soap (. . .) No, I can't say I'm surprised either, (. . .) The what about putting the pieces of paper into alphanumeric order? (. . .) Oh, well. You might say that the two are equally important, or even that one is no good without the other. If one of the pieces of paper is in the right alpha but the wrong numerical then it has been misfiled. Similarly, a piece of the paper that is numerically correct but alpha incorrect – I wouldn't be able as a manager to say that that piece of the paper has been correctly filed. The Recruitment Consultant would get off the phone none the wiser, still with the same problem to solve.

The bear is in the office. He is in front of his computer. He clicks one window open and looks at the number in it. He clicks open another window, moves his mouse into one of the blank fields and types in the number. He moves the mouse and clicks a button and the screen refreshes to reveal the field blank again. The bear switches windows again and looks at the number. He clicks open another window. He moves his mouse. He runs his claws through the coarse scruff on top of his head. He gets up. He goes to the toilets and enters a stall. He puts his head against the cold formica side panel. He feels his sinew stir. He shuts his eyes. There is so much of the day left.

The bear is stood on a pallet on a wet concrete patch. Another man calls him. He gets down off the pallet and walks towards the open end of an articulated lorry trailer. It is cold. His jacket is bunched around his throat. He looks at the man inside the lorry and the man looks back. The bear grips the bottom of the refrigerator and begins to take the strain of it, hard and coarse against his palms. The man steadies the top. The bear lowers one side of the leaning fridge to the ground and lets the top tilt into him, taking its weight until it is righted. The other man turns away and rubs his eyes with the heels of his hands. The bear looks around. He can't see the forklift. There are eight more fridges in the van. It is getting dark. The yellow forklift comes out of the warehouse and the man driving it is laughing.

The character was a farmer. You could tell by his clothes, dark green wax jacket, hat, wellingtons, his sideburns, his stick. You could tell this but, still, he lived in the town and didn't live alone. He lived with the philosopher and he lived with the invalid. He lived with the DJ and with the clown. When they all put their clothes on and walked down the steep hill to the pub and ordered coloured drinks and sat at the big table together, it felt like they could be in LA, or Vegas. Maybe even Paris, or Egypt. The farmer liked, on certain days, to walk through the city, into the centre and further on, down to the train station which was at the bottom of a hill. Behind the station were big grey blocks of flats. Funnily enough, it was the clown that the farmer had known the longest. On those days the farmer would go into the station, fold his big coat over his arm, lean his stick up against the wall and think to himself, I could get a train back out to the fields, get it going again.

The DJ was another type all together. Though, in a different way, he was a similar type. The DJ didn't mind being in a city which had so few good clubs for him to DJ at. He thought, with the new technology, why should I be limited to playing raves in just one place? I can sit in my bedroom and play out to raves in Stockholm and Tokyo, London, Africa, New Zealand. Thoughts like these contented the DJ.

✦

Unsurprisingly, the philosopher and the clown got on well. Sometimes it was hard to tell the two of them apart. They wore each other's clothes, they made the same jokes, but they were different people. The clown was tall and spindly while the philosopher had a beard. No. The other way round.

The invalid was another member of the group and, by virtue of being the only woman, was something of a focal point. It was often the invalid who cast the deciding vote over whether to go to the pub that night or stay in with the telly. Or whatever else it was that they may have been unable to decide. It was a position of power, it was a position of some loneliness, some despair. But the invalid neither enjoyed nor disliked it. The invalid had a lot of problems. For one, she couldn't work. None of the others worked either, but the subtle difference, as the philosopher once pointed out, to the clown's delight, was that the invalid couldn't work, whereas the rest of them just didn't. Hence her name, hence her status. Was the philosopher right?

Their house was always banging. The closer you got to the DJ's room, the louder the beats got, but you could always hear them, wherever you were. The group liked nothing better than to take a picnic to the park. The DJ would bring his boombox and blast out the tunes. The invalid would sit in the middle, scoffing the foul-smelling sandwiches and uttering words like 'rot', 'slump', 'slop'. The philosopher would laugh at something in the paper, pass it to the clown, who would laugh too. While the farmer would plant his stick in the soft earth under the rug, look past the nests of houses that made up the town and over into the always visible hills, think about getting it going again.

The Recruitment Consultant woke up. Her eyelids were stuck together with sleep. Her nose was blocked. It was cold in the room. In the bathroom, she brushed her teeth and spat. There was blood in what she spat. She brushed her tongue and gagged. She had a song in her head. She spat a yellow mucous into the sink and washed it away with the tap. The milk was off so she had to skip breakfast. Her trousers were cold on her legs when she put them on. And the blouse, too, was cold. In the mirror, her eyes were red, puffy. She regarded herself in the mirror before leaving for work. All she could think of was the song.

The bear goes to a public lecture on modern horror writing. Or that is what it purported to be. The supposed lecturer takes to the lectern and begins reciting. What he is saying, it seems to this bear to be nothing more than recycled postmodern jargon, and entirely meaningless. The people sitting around the bear are listening hard and taking it all in. After a time, from the back of the hall, behind everyone, comes a person dressed in a very convincing bear costume. It runs down the aisle, up onto the stage and slams into the aghast-looking lecturer, knocking him down. It gazes out over the audience. There are screams. It then drags the lecturer behind the curtain and there are noises. The curtains rustle dramatically. All the organisers and ushers seem to have disappeared. Moments later, it reappears, its synthetic face and paws bloodstained. It runs back down the aisle, not looking at anyone. The bear half-rises and turns to see the person in the bear costume run out the back door, then slumps back into his seat. Nothing happens for some minutes and everyone stays still. Their whispers are agitated, but no one speaks to the bear. He is on his own. The house lights go up suddenly and, when it's clear nothing else is going to happen, people begin to numbly file out.

It turns out the whole thing was a set-up. The bear finds this out a few weeks later. The audience reactions were being filmed while the stunt took place. The footage is shown in an art gallery for one month as part of an exhibition subtitled *New Visions of Shared Spaces*. The bear goes down one afternoon and sees himself looking bemused, then anxious, scared and then confused. Sees his own head turn and watch the person in the bear suit leaving the auditorium. At this point the camera zooms abruptly towards the back of the bear's head and it is alarming for him to see himself as he turns back round, still in focus, falls into his chair and stares, black eyes creased and small.

The noise of the dogs in the waterlogged park behind her room woke the Recruitment Consultant. It was night time. She went to her window, feeling the fur on her teeth, her tongue, the crust in the corners of her eyes. With the heel of her hand she worked her eyeballs around. The park was shrouded in a weird light and the dogs were like little tufts of hair scattered across a big dark leg. The grass was no colour she'd seen before and there were traffic noises, sirens and shouting from the other side of the house. The dog noises were louder. It was as if the whole night had loomed closer to the window. In the air was rain, thin and sharp and miserly, and the dogs made splashes that she could hear faintly when the traffic sounds died away. Then there was shouting and a crash and Simon ran into the room and told her to come look. His room was lit up all orange by the house across the road, which was on fire. In front of the burning house, standing in the waterlogged grass, were three men and an overweight, squat woman whose hair looked moulded on. This was the group that lived there and they stood with their backs to Simon and the Recruitment Consultant, watching their house burn down. The fire had begun in the kitchen, started by the other that lived there. He was already dead and charred, lying and burning on the lino along with saucepans and cutlery, food, condiments, plates.

◆

Simon and the Recruitment Consultant stood on the wet path in front of their house, narrow enough that they each had one foot in the wet grass. The firemen had pushed the group back onto the pavement. People were coming out of their houses to stand and watch the fire. The wind, which fanned the flames that now broke through the roof and surged through the windows, spilling breaking glass, and the rain, which was growing heavier, reminded them of the cold. The house brayed and popped. Heat hummed from behind the door frame. Further down the street there was shouting. There were more sirens. Under the Recruitment Consultant's feet and shoes the path was hot. Brittle ash fell around them and turned gooey in the rain. Everyone stood for a long time watching. The wind was picking up; there was a booming in the distance. Dogs howled. The firemen could not get near the house.

The Recruitment Consultant's clothes were sticky underneath with sweat, clammy on top from the rain. She was flushed. The police were talking to one of the men from the house; he carried a stick, he had sideburns, he was wearing a wax jacket. He turned and looked back at the Recruitment Consultant, his face an orange globe of pain.

The bear is in the pub with his girlfriend's father. It had been intended for it to be just the two of them, but when they get to the pub, they run into two of the father's friends. The father is a dentist. He is a man and he has a big pink face. His friends, likewise. The dentist is called Clive. The dentist puts his drink down and, looking at the bear, he begins to speak. It's a fucking gamble being a dentist. Here. Distracted, the dentist points at the folded paper in the bear's bag. You on the crossword? Here you go . . . Two down, Flaubert, easy. The dentist picks up the paper and starts filling in the clue with angled capitals. Flaubert is incorrect. The bear, drinking his drink, looks at the dentist. Fucking gamble, as I was saying. I had this girl in a few days ago, I seen her a few times before, she was just in for a checkup. Beautiful teeth she had, not a thing wrong with them. Anyway, I'm poking around and, uh, the dentist picks up his pint and swigs from it, he then cocks the pen which he still holds in the direction of the bear. His friends follow the pen with their eyes. They have pork-scratching skin and bad breath. She's lying on the chair, just there like where you are now and I'm having a go in her mouth, y'know, when I notice that her skirt – it was a short skirt, floaty sort of material – has ridden up. This is the gamble, because, she's lying there with her mouth open, eyes closed, but the position of her hands, it almost looks like she'd done it on purpose. You know, pulled the skirt up? The dentist sits back and drinks. The bear drinks. Shit, man. What did you do? goes one of the two friends. It is very loud in the pub. The dentist leans in; he is still looking at the bear. He has an incredulous look on his face. He turns to the guy, then he turns back to the bear, still with the incredulous look. What the fuck do you think I did, Andy? Andy shrugs. Fuck all, is what I did. That's the gamble. Sometimes you do, sometimes you don't. What I generally do, if it happens more than once – that's the clue – I rest a hand gently on their thigh as I'm working, gauge the response and go from there. But like I say, it's a fucking lottery. Pick the wrong numbers and you could land up in court, in jail, lose your job, lose your wife and kids. You got to play the system. You got to have rules. He grins at them one by one. Fuck, goes Andy. Fucking hell. The dentist drains his pint and looks down the glass, surprised that there is nothing left in it. He turns the paper onto the back page and runs his eyes over it. The bear feels itchy under his clothes. It is so loud in there. Another drink? the dentist asks and they all nod. He goes to the bar.

Ever since the bear saw Sarah for the first time he had wanted to fuck her. He was starting some office job and he was being shown round the office for the first time. That's when he first saw her. They were introduced briefly, flatly. He was Regis, she was Sarah. The old woman showing the bear around said, This is Sarah, and she just said Hi and smiled. The bear thought she looked good. He sat at a desk some distance away, but he could see her profile. He could see her right hand on the mouse, gently moving it, clicking that mouse. That's what she did. Surreptitiously he would watch her face and see it move in moments pregnant with erotic tension. He loves to watch her talk, see her face change from thoughtfulness into delight, from mock annoyance to sarcasm. He loves to watch her mouth move, form words, teeth lingering against her bottom lip as she emphasises a syllable. These small movements, it seems to the bear, are a microcosm of the larger movements of her whole frame, they are characteristic.

He loves her languidness, the way she sits with her chin in her hand and stares off beyond her monitor, her free hand playing gently with the mouse. He loves her sudden flurries of activity, how she attacks the keyboard, her brow furrowed, her lips pursed. On the days when she has bare arms, he likes to look at her arms. He waits impatiently for the times when she stretches, her breasts rising and flattening and her top riding up a little, revealing her round white stomach's bulge. Every movement she makes excites him in some way and he spends a lot of time in this job looking at her. He peeks out from behind his monitor when she gets up to get a glass of water or a cup of coffee. He watches the movement of her buttocks as she walks towards the sink, as she turns on the tap. He looks at her tits as she returns to her desk, cup in hand, watches them as she turns and sits back down, in profile to him again.

They don't talk much really. The bear is not awkward around her and nor is she particularly shy, but they are just a little far from each other to hold a conversation comfortably across the office. It is just chat, when they talk. Is there an element of flirtation? It's hard to say. She is always nice to everyone. He watches her fingers on the keyboard; she is able to type very quickly. She wears no ring, but she does talk sometimes about a boyfriend. The bear doesn't mind that though. Such as his desire is, he has no intention of acting upon it. He likes her to remain abstract, distant, meaningfully distant. His desire is bound up in expectation and delay. When he arrives at the office, he anticipates what she will be wearing that day. He relishes warmer days when she sheds jumpers and cardigans, reveals armpits, neck, shoulders. Each day brings a new spectrum of movement, new fabrics on her skin, new colours against the flush of her cheek and the swish of thin hair that falls and splays against her shoulders.

The bear asks her sometimes to help him with something

on his computer, or to have a look at some unusual file or piece of information. He saves these up and waits until she is the nearest person, then asks. She walks to his desk and leans over him. He smells her chewing-gum breath, feels her softness. Their arms would glance, perhaps their legs would even touch briefly. On one occasion she was standing opposite the bear, he was sitting at his computer, they were talking about something. A drop of saliva flew from her mouth and landed on the bear's forearm. He continued saying whatever he was saying, but he felt it land and looked down and saw it glistening there against his coarse pink skin. He felt its coolness. He looked up at her. She was tidying her hair with her index finger, pushing it away from her eyes. The conversation petered out and she returned to her desk. He looked at the wet dot on his arm. A small shiver ran through him. Carefully, lightly, he touched it with his tongue. There was no taste to it. And yet he seemed to feel it inside himself.

The office becomes a site of erotic possibility. Every chance of proximity, every touch of fingers or hint of scent is charged for the bear. There is something about her body angled at the photocopier, the density of her calf muscles leaning against the frame of the machine. He would save his photocopying up if he could, until she was going over. Or he would try to pre-empt when she was about to go and go himself before she got up. Would he have noticed her out on the street, if they weren't in an office? He did consider that. It is worth consideration. But he reasons that the substance of his affection for her is bound up in the

environment he sees her in, in the possibility she repre-
sents of transgression, of freedom, of joy.

One evening he is invited out to the pub with some of the
guys from the office, an offer he usually politely declines,
but since she is going, he goes too. It is a Friday. They go
and sit around a crowded table in a loud pub. This bear
feels ideologically opposed to pubs. They are sitting opposite each other, but she is talking to someone else. Another
guy is telling the bear about a goal he had once scored
during a five-a-side football match. He just got the ball
around the halfway line, he didn't normally go on runs but
he saw some space, did a little jink round the defender and
then just blasted it into the top corner. People were talking
about it afterwards. It had been a great goal. The bear nods.
He moves, as if casually, the side of his shoe against her
foot. He does it without appearing to notice. She does not
move her foot away or appear to notice at all. The bear
looks down at his big shoe touching her tiny little one. He
looks up at her. She is sipping a red-coloured drink from a
bottle. She is nodding at the girl next to her who is saying
something about a film. The bear sips some of a beer. The
guy who had told the bear about the goal he once scored
is now telling the same story to someone across the table.
When he jinked, you know, he didn't just drop his shoulder, he kind of flicked it past the defender with the outside
of his foot. With five-a-side it's not like being on a big pitch,
you don't have the space, it's more about close control and
short passing. It's a skilful game in its way. The man jostles
the bear with his elbows as he describes arcs of motion,

tactical manoeuvres, the path of the ball from his foot into the goal. First his hands are the ball, then they are the goal-keeper's hands and his face is the goalkeeper's face gazing at the ball as it soars past him into the top corner. He put just the right amount of curl on it, any more and it would have gone wide, any less and it would have been an easy one for the keeper. What a great goal. The bear's foot is still in the same position and so is hers. If this had been in the office, he would have barely been able to contain himself. But here in the pub he feels very little. He looks up at her and she is talking to no one. She smiles at him, flattens her lips together and raises her eyebrows in a gesture that is both conciliatory and conspiratorial, both inviting and indifferent, both bland and affecting. Their eyes meet for a second, but then they both turn away. The bear scratches his chin. He has been thinking about growing a beard. She sips her drink. He sips his. The guy next to the bear is saying something about a film. Apparently, without giving away the ending, there's this really good scene where this dog, right? Anyway you have to know that the dog isn't really a dog, he's really this guy and he's kind of been trapped in the body of the dog by terrorists for knowing too many federal secrets. Anyway, the dog is trying to contact his old boss, who is like the one guy he can trust. Or that's what you think anyway when you're watching it. We see the dog like go into his house, the boss's house, I mean, and the dog is barking and jumping up at this guy and he won't leave him alone at all. Eventually the boss looks into the dog's eyes and he's like, Sammy? Is that really you? Sammy is the name of the guy who is trapped in the body of the dog. And the dog is all barking and nodding. Anyway the boss has retired and there's the implication that he's pretty much lost whatever it was that made him a great boss. He has this train set which he is playing with before the dog comes in and when the dog is scraping at the door we see him pick up a newspaper off the mat with a headline about the political situation, but he barely even seems to register it, he just sort of throws the paper down. But seeing Sammy like that gets him all fired up and passionate. He agrees to follow the dog. And the audience, we're all thinking that the dog's going to lead him to the base of the bad guys, who are terrorists who have infiltrated the White House. The dog leads him on this long walk, like through a forest and over a massive hill and eventually they come to this town. And they're walking through these streets in a pretty run-down place; there's all homeless people around and smashed-up cars. So we're thinking this is the perfect place for the ter-rorist hideout. Except then the dog stops at this doorway and starts barking excitedly and the boss goes, Is this the place, Sammy? And the dog is barking more and more and looks really excited, except then the camera pans upwards towards a sign which says, Dog Food Factory. And then we realise that not only have they turned Sammy into a dog, but they have also taken away his brain. Only then does the boss realise that he wasn't even particularly fired up when he was following the dog, not compared to how fired up he is now, and he resolves to take those terrorist bastards out. Anyway, it's a really good scene. It does sound like a pretty good scene. The bear looks away from the guy and towards her. She is laughing at something, possibly she is laughing

24

at that scene. The bear had found it sad rather than funny. It had made him want to see that film. The bear sips his drink. All the erotic tension of the silence of the office has been broken. Their feet are still touching but she is just a girl.

The bear is at work. Again, he is at work. He is watching her typing some document. Despite his indifference to her at the pub, his ardour for her at work has not been diminished. Her fingers, that's what he is looking at. On her wrists she is wearing a few plastic bangles. She is wearing a powder-blue short-sleeved blouse. It bunches at the sleeve and has a white lace trim. It is a girlish item. It looks a little tight on her, but good. She has it unbuttoned low, and though the fabric clings, when she is at the right angle and the bear is at the right angle he can observe a section of her black bra strap and a portion of her left breast. He looks at his screen then looks back at her; she is turned away from him. Her hair is up today and the bear observes her neck and her shoulders under the blue blouse. She turns again, lifts a glass of water with her right hand and drinks it all down. The bear watches the curvature of her throat and chin, how it rises to swallow and returns. She rubs her left eye with her left index finger. She uncrosses her legs. He sees all this. She types a word and then deletes it. She types another. She yawns and stretches out, her arms straight and high and the bear observes the lightly puckered skin of her shaved armpit. So as not to be silent for too long, the bear types some nonsense into his keyboard. It appears on the screen in a long unbroken line. Just letters.

He highlights it all and then deletes it. He doesn't have a single thing to do today. He looks vaguely around the office. People working, people talking. She shuffles in her chair, she seems restless. She frowns. She clicks open a different document and reads through it, frowning. She leans back and sighs. She gets up out of her chair. She picks up the glass. She goes to the water cooler and fills the glass. Some guy walking past her says something to her and she replies with a half-smile. He goes. The bear sees her roll her eyes. She looks at her watch. She puts the glass down and sits down. She looks at her watch again. The bear notices the manager come through the door. He is a man with grey hair. His suit is too big for him and his eyes are watery. He goes over to her and perches on the edge of her desk. He mumbles something quietly to her. She nods, she bites her lip. She moves the mouse around. She searches through folders and opens some document. He glances at it, he says something again and nods. She nods. He puts his hand on her shoulder and looks around at the screen. He says something and laughs. She nods and smiles. The bear notices how the manager's eyes keep dipping towards her chest, how he shifts around on the desk to see better. She does not appear to notice as she moves through this document, making comments, pointing things out. He nods and smiles. He gets up, he starts to move away but then returns, leaning over her left side, his right arm stretched across and lingering on her right shoulder. He points at something. Their faces are close. She wriggles a little to get away but he moves with it automatically, naturally, staying close to her. He is continuing to mumble to her. The bear hears her say Yes. Finally the manager stands, moves his hand down from her shoulder onto the small of her back, which he pats. He turns away from her. The bear sees her frown. He comes over to the bear. Regis, is it? he says, Could I have a word with you, please? Without waiting for the bear's response he turns and walks away towards his office. The bear sees what is going to happen. He stands up and follows the manager into the small windowless office which has a chart on the wall and a desk and two chairs.

The manager is sitting down at his desk. He clicks the mouse a few times on his keyboard before he invites the bear to sit down. He is a nobody. He starts to talk: Uh . . . Regis, he goes, right. Now, uh, you've been here for what? Just over two months? And . . . Well, I've been in touch with the agency this morning about this. I, uh, would you mind if I just nipped out for a glass of water? The bear shrugs. The manager gets up and leaves the office. The bear sits and looks around. There is a picture of a kid in a frame on the desk. What an ugly kid. It is 11:28. The bear waits. It takes a full fifteen minutes for the manager to return and when he does he has no water. Sorry about that, uh, I bumped into Dave from . . . well, you probably won't know Dave actually, he's another one of the managers. Anyway, as I was saying, I was on the phone to Lucy at the agency this morning . . . Do you know Lucy? She's new, apparently. We were both saying that your work here has been very good. Sheila has also told me that you've got through everything very quickly. So, uh, well done for that. There is a pause where the manager shuffles through a few pieces of paper on his desk and clicks the mouse a few more times. The bear sits silently looking at him. He's seen what's coming. He's waiting for it. As you know we're under pressure to meet certain budgetary targets. Part of the profitability of the bank is to do with trying to cut costs at every level where possible. The decision has been made to not continue your contract with us at the moment. The bear stands. He rubs his chin. He is still thinking about that beard. You, uh . . . I'm not quite . . . goes the manager. The bear does not sit down but stays there, his bulk up against the desk, his head grazing the ceiling tiles. You understand, continues the man, that this is nothing to do with you. As I say, I've spoken to the agency this morning and as far as they're concerned there's no problems, they're happy for you to continue to work for them. I suggest you pop in some time this after-noon, you're already in town and . . . The bear shuts his eyes and smacks his forehead with the palm of his hand. He looks hard at the manager sitting there. The manager gets up and offers his hand to the bear. Well, he says, thanks for all you've done. I hope you've enjoyed it, uh . . . The bear looks down at the hand for a long, awkward moment. The manager lets it slowly go limp. He begins to withdraw it and then thrusts it out again, looking up at the bear hopefully. The bear continues to look at the hand. Then he looks at the man in front of him. The bear turns around, he leaves the office. He walks back to his desk. He gets his stuff. He looks over at Sarah. She is typing something. It's the last time he'll see her, this way at least. He leaves.

On one occasion a school group had scheduled a visit to the agency and the Recruitment Consultant had been asked to show them around and answer any of their questions. The group came in, about twenty twelve- or thirteen- or fourteen- or eleven-year-olds and their teacher, a man. The Recruitment Consultant was just about to lean across her desk and say to a colleague, Gemma, while spinning her monitor round to show a picture something probably like Look at this young socialite's new haircut. I like neither it, nor the cut of the dress she is wearing, nor, to be perfectly frank, her. She was about to do that when the kids walked in and she remembered that she had forgotten all about their visit.

She stood up from her chair, patted down her skirt, leant down and clicked closed the celebrity gossip website and her email and eBay and a site with discounts on bags and a newspaper website and then walked over to greet the kids. Hi, kids, she said, I'm Carol and we're here today to put all of you kids into jobs. Now, which of you wants to work as a baked beans, baked potato, mashed potato and sausage distributor at the service station canteen near junction twelve?! She paused and the kids looked around at the office, which had a green carpet and computers in it. Only joking! she resumed. That was just a little joke. I'm really here to show you all about what goes on at a Recruitment

Agency. Although that job that I just mentioned is a real job and you guys are probably too young, but if any of your big brothers or sisters have expressed an interest in working on the motorway or in service station catering then get them to give me a call. If your parents are interested then they can call too. Though they mostly want dynamic younger people for the role. It can be quite demanding, especially on weekends and bank holidays.

Now, what I thought we'd do is that I'd show you what I do right from the start. Right from the point at which someone, someone maybe just like one or more of you, walks through our door there looking for a job and right up to the point where we actually offer them a job. OK? Now the first thing we do with that person is sit them down, we maybe offer them a tea or coffee and we just have a chat with them to find out what they're all about, what kind of thing they are interested in doing, what their skills are et cetera. So would somebody like to volunteer to pretend to be that person and the rest of you can watch and ask any questions that you might want to have. OK? So who wants to volunteer? Huh? Anybody? Come on, don't be shy now. You? No? Come on! Anyone? You? No? You? OK? OK? Huh? You? Come on, sit down there on this chair now. OK? Now, what's your name?

– Gary, Miss.

– You don't have to call me Miss, I'm not a teacher. Now, what's your surname, Gary?

– Roper, Miss. There was laughter from the kids. The teacher frowned.

– I don't see what you are laughing at, said the Recruitment Consultant. I don't really . . . what is so funny?

– It's because Groper, Miss, said one of the kids.

– Don't call me Miss. What? Groper? I don't . . . Groper? Are you? You're not. There's nothing wrong with him, is there, Mister umm? She turned to the teacher.

– Edwards. No. There's nothing wrong with Gary. He's making a joke. Gee Roper, you see. It spells Groper.

– What spells Groper? Groper? I don't . . . Wait . . . He's . . . so is Groper not his name then? I mean, is Gary not his name or?

– Gary is his name. His real surname is Blake. But Roper plus the Gee makes the name spell Groper. Do you see now? Some of the kids were in stitches by this point. This was the best thing to happen to them in ages, really.

– Right, right. I still don't . . . Oh no, wait. Yes. Gee Roper, Groper. I see. They go on different parts of the form here, so I . . . You don't usually think of them together really. So what is . . . let me look at this form here. This is the form we fill in, by the way, kids. So, wait, now I've put you in as Groper but you're, let me. Now what is . . . Gary is your name, right?

– Yes, Miss.

– Don't call me Miss. And what is your surname, Gary, if it's not Roper, ahahaha.

– Angster, Miss. A-n-g-s-t-a.

– Don't call me Miss. All right, now . . . what are you laughing at now?

– It's the same joke again, answered the teacher, this time it spells Gangster.

– It spells what? Grandma? How can it, there's no. . .

– . . . Gangster. Gang . . . ster.

– Gangster? What even? But it has no R on the end . . . Oh right, now I see it, I suppose. Now, Gary . . . what is his surname, Mister um?

– Edwards.

– OK, Gary Edwards. . .

– . . . No, Edwards is my name, his is Blake.

– All right, now, Gary Blake, that is all very funny and all very well and good, but if you were in a real job interview situation and you tried to make a joke like that do you think it would make a very good impression on me, the person who is going to be working on your behalf to try to find you a job? Is that what you think?

– Can I have a tea, Miss?

– Don't call me Miss. What?

– Cause you said that when you interview people they get to have a cup of tea and that, Miss.

– Well, I don't – don't call me Miss – I don't think really . . . the machine is out of order today anyway, I think.

– But that woman there has a cup of tea. She just made it, Miss.

– Don't call me Miss. We don't have time to make tea at the moment, perhaps later. Now, uh, Gary, you haven't made too good an impression to begin with but we can see past that if you answer these next questions well. Now what. . .

– . . . But I don't want no job, Miss.

– Don't call me Miss. What do you mean? Look, just for the purposes of this exercise so I can show you what would happen if you did want a job, can we go through these questions now? Gary looked perplexed. He looked round at his classmates who also looked perplexed. The Recruitment Consultant continued.

– What would you say your skills were, Gary? There was a long pause before Gary answered.

– I don't know, Miss.

– Don't call me Miss. What are you good at, Gary? Are you a hard worker? Are you punctual? Gary looked increasingly perplexed.

– I'm fast, Miss.

– Can you not call me Miss, please? OK, good, you're fast at what? Typing?

– Nah, Miss, I'm fast at, you know, running. I got the year eight record at sports day.

– Well . . . OK, and how do you think you could use that skill in a business context?

– What's context, Miss?

– Context is . . . well, how could you apply your fast running to a job you might be doing? Gary thought for a moment and, smiling, answered.

– I could run really fast away from it and they couldn't catch me, Miss.

– Don't call me Miss, please. Now what? I think you've misunderstood what I'm . . . What I'm getting at is in what sphere could your fast running be put to best use in a business environment?

– Well, because, like, I don't want to do a job, Miss, I could run away from it so fast that they couldn't catch me.

– Look, Gary, eventually you will have to get a job to support yourself and your family, if you have one, so let's just assume that that time has come and you're in here interviewing for that job and so ... do you have other skills besides being fast?

– Yeah.

– Good, that's good. What are they?

– I don't know, like, I completed the new GTA in like two weeks not even using the cheats. It only took me like one attempt to do the last mission.

– Nah, it never, interrupted another boy.

– Chut up, man, chut up, retorted Gary, I got the AK47 from in that room, and the health. Anyway, you ain't even completed it because you ain't even got no Xbox. There was a general muttering throughout the office. The issue of whether this kid hadn't even got no Xbox was a contentious one.

– Right, continued the Recruitment Consultant. OK, for now we'll leave that area. Gary, what would you say your weaknesses are?

– What?

– Your weaknesses. What areas aren't you so good in?

– Why do you want to know that, Miss?

– Don't call me Miss. Well, we want to know that because we want a rounded picture of the kind of person you are so we can find you the most suitable job possible. So. . .?

– Wait, so you want me to tell you what my weaknesses are?

– That's right.

– Except, I'm supposed to be here trying to get a job, trying to help my family and whatever, so if I told you that I was lazy or that I got fired from like my last ten jobs then you ain't gonna give me no job, are you?

– Well . . . that's very shrewd of you, Gary. Well done! Kids, what Gary has managed to do is see through the question in a very clever way. The point of the question is not for him to tell us that he's not good at things, it's a way of us getting him to tell us about something that at first glance might seem negative but, once he has fully explained it it actually comes out looking like a positive. Do you think he can manage it? Gary, can you?

– Wait a minute. I've got to say something so that it sounds like a weakness but really it's not a weakness because if I actually told you about a weakness then I wouldn't get no job?

– Well, something like that is . . .

– Because like if I actually needed a job to support my family or if I had kids or whatever then you pulling some trick question like that is straight bullshit. The Recruitment Consultant pulled a face. She looked up at Mr Edwards but he just stared back at her. He looked at her stonily. The kids were not laughing at this point.

– Right, OK, she said. We'll move on, shall we? Can you give me an example, Gary, of a time when you motivated someone that you weren't managerially responsible for? Gary looked at her impassively.

– What?

– I said, can you give me an example of when you motivated someone that you weren't managerially responsible for? What I mean is can you give me an example of a time when you, Gary, have motivated someone?

– Motivated them to do what, Miss?

– Don't call me Miss. Well, anything, something at work, er, at school even or even in your personal life.

– I don't really . . . tend to do that.

– Well, you see, Gary, what I'm trying to ask you is how you are likely to respond to the challenges that regularly come up in the workplace and one of those might be to get someone to do something. I'm looking for you to display some competency in this area because it's such a big part of most jobs.

– Well, like I say, I don't really do that, so . . .

– I'm really going to press you on this one, you must be able to think of something that you've done at home, maybe if you have a younger brother or sister you've helped out at home or a friend here that you've motivated to join an after-school club or something like that.

– I don't think . . . I don't see why you need to know that, though, Miss.

– Don't call me Miss. I . . . well. What it is is I'm trying to do is build up a holistic picture of your skills and interests and it's only once I've done that that I can see what jobs you might be suitable for.

– What's holistic, Miss?

– Holistic means if you're employable or not.

– So, like, what kind of jobs do you have here?

– Well. We're straying from the point a little, I think, so . . .

– But, like, if I'm having an interview then I need to know what job it's for.

– Well, currently the roles that we have in are mostly clerical admin-based positions, so your main tasks would be things like filing, photocopying, maybe some data entry.

– What's clerical, Miss?

– Clerical is where. Well. To be clerical is to be good at filing. That's what clerical means. It's a descriptive word. Are you clerical, Graham?

– What?

– Sorry, Gary. I meant Gary.

– What is filing, Miss?

– Don't call me Miss. Filing. What it is is it would be, for example, if I gave you a list of the forms of all the people who are registered here and asked you to put them in alphabetical order and then put them in a cupboard. That entire process is filing. That whole thing from start to finish, what you're doing there is filing. Do you understand?

– Nah, not really, Miss.

– What about that don't you understand?

– I just don't get why you would need to do that.

– Well, we need accurate and easily accessible records so that we can get to whatever information we might need without . . .

– Yeah, but like why would you have all your forms out in one go?

– I don't understand what you're asking me, Gary.

– So, like you give me all these forms and I have to put them in order, but why are they out of the cupboard?

– Well, that's just an example of what filing is, Gary, I'm not saying that this is what you have to do, I'm just saying it's something like what you would have to do in a clerical job.

– It sounds boring, Miss.

– On the contrary, Gary, having a good filing system is integral to the smooth running of any office. Let me tell you something, Gary, and you children, everyone in an organisation is important right from the boss of the whole company, the CEO, down to the cleaner who cleans the boss's toilet. They are all important and a company can't run without them. They . . . yes, what? A girl had her hand up.

– Miss, what is CEO, Miss?

– CEO is Latin. It's hard to translate but it means something like a big boss or master of something. Anyway, as I was saying. What was I saying?

– You were saying about how a CEO is lacking, Miss, said the girl.

– No, not . . . don't call me Miss, please. CEO is Latin. Not lacking. Latin. Latin is a language that the ancient Greeks spoke and it's the language that all philosophy must be written in. A lot of business terms come from this language. Filing, for example, which we were talking about earlier, that comes from a Latin word, 'Filo', meaning someone who loves to file things or someone who likes putting things in order. It's also, uh, there's also a type of pastry named after this word. This pastry has a lot of layers, like pieces of paper in a filing cabinet. That's probably where that's from. Anyway I was, uh. The Recruitment Consultant glanced up at the teacher who was looking up at her from behind the children. His expression was hard to read. I was saying that the cleaner is as important as any other member of staff in any organisation, that's what I was saying. And it's true! Do you think a CEO has time to clean his own toilet? No. He does not. He does not have time to clean his own toilet. And just like he might employ someone like you to file papers that he's signed, he will also employ someone to clean his toilet. And the company simply could not run without clean toilets or proper filing systems. They are all as important as each other, the clerical assistant, the cleaner and the CEO. A company needs all of them to function properly. Do you understand what I'm saying to you, uh, Gary?

– Yes, Miss.

Now, Gary, let's get on with the questions. Where do you see yourself in five years' time?

– I'll still be at school, Miss.

– Yes, OK, we've already established that. What I'm wanting from you is how you think your life will be different in five years' time?

– I dunno, Miss. I'll probably smoke. The children laughed.

– Right. OK. Right. Now, Gary. Now. What you have to remember is that when you're in a job interview situation it's not a situation where making jokes is appropriate. What you have to remember is that the person interviewing you has the power to give you a job or withhold a job from you. In this particular situation, I am the one who has that power. I interview you and if you say too many things that I find inappropriate then it won't be possible for me to put you forward for jobs. It's up to you to learn how to behave in this type of situation. She looked at the teacher's face. It's up to you to learn because it doesn't matter how good you are, it doesn't matter how capable you are of performing whatever tasks a job entails, if you can't sit down in front of me and look right and say the right things then I'm not going to give you a job. People come in here, some people, they come in here and they've got all the qualifications in the world. Do you think any of those people aren't capable of doing ninety per cent of the jobs we have in here? They are, of course they are. Most people are capable of most jobs. And people come in here and I can see that they're capable, I can see that they can do most of the jobs we get in here, but if they aren't dressed properly, or if they don't come up with the answers I want to hear when I ask them questions, then they don't get a job from me. So you have to learn what those answers are and you have to learn the correct way of presenting yourself. And your CV has to look right. It doesn't matter if it's not true, as long as it looks right. If you get those things right, then you'll get a job, and once you get a job, if you want to stay in that job then it doesn't really matter how you behave, within reason of course. Now, Gary, she said, though she was still looking at the teacher, if you look at any office, if you go to any office anywhere and really look at what people are doing there and how those people do what they do, let me tell you what you'll see. You'll see routine incompetence, you'll see laziness, you'll see time being wasted, you'll see bullying, you'll see prejudice. You'll see all these things. It doesn't matter what the office does, or where it is, if you go in there you'll see all these things. Job interviews are one way of ensuring that this can continue, so that on paper everyone looks capable and competent, whether they are or aren't. If you go into any office what you'll see are not necessarily the best people for the jobs they are doing but people who are able to appear in certain situations, of which the job interview is one example, to be best equipped to do them. I am a custodian of this process. I make sure it continues. I make sure it works. And it does work, and it's not going to change. OK? OK, Gary? Gary was silent. When I ask someone a question at an interview there is so much behind the question that that person has to think about. I'm often surprised by how easily people answer these questions which contain multitudes. The density of information that they have to consider and convey, it often makes me think. But people learn it, and your children will learn it, eventually, and it will become as automatic to you as flinching when someone moves to strike you. Now I think we can . . . The teacher stood up and interrupted. I think, he said, we've run out of time. The Recruitment Consultant looked at her watch, But it's, uh, it's only twenty past. I thought you were . . . But the teacher was already gathering the children into lines, shepherding them out the door, nodding a curt thanks. The Recruitment Consultant sat there in her green chair.

The bear is in the men's. He is at the urinal. He looks ahead. His frame is vast and his centre of gravity is low. From behind the walls comes the noise of water moving through pipes. All the stalls are occupied. The bear can see feet under the walls of the nearest one, black trainers, soles turned inwards. On the other side of the bear, the door opens. A man comes in, he glances at the bear. He looks over at the stalls, he sees they are all occupied. He comes and stands next to the bear and undoes his jeans. The man pulls his dick out. The man spits into the urinal trough. The bear looks ahead. He feels the man turning to look at him, he feels that. He continues to look ahead. The water moves through the pipes and there is noise. The men's is of an older design. The urinal is one long trough, with semi-cylindrical tiles sloping down to one metal grate. The trough is set slightly below the floor, the lip of which is made of brown tiles. The rest of the floor has grey tiles. There are small rectangular windows high up; the glass in them is yellow. The bear has no notion of what those windows would look out on, if you could climb up, if you could see through the yellow glass. He has no notion of where in the building he is. The man is not going, he isn't pissing. The bear glances down at him. Ugh, says the man, and then shortly afterwards he says, Ugh. He gives a sigh. He looks at the bear. He is shaking his head. I can't go, he goes, I can't go while you're here. He steps away from the urinal, turns and does up his trousers. He goes to the sink and rinses the tips of his fingers. He dries his fingers on his jeans. He leaves the room. The bear finishes and goes to wash his hands.

The Recruitment Consultant and her colleague, a man called Alan, were walking on the outskirts of a city, towards a hotel where a conference was being held. Their taxi driver had assured them this was the road. It was drizzling. They were walking in the scurf at the side of a busy road. Behind a hedgerow and a fence and some trees they could see what they were sure were the grounds of the hotel and even, where the hedge broke up a little, one brown wall of it, a glimpse of a window frame. They trudged on. They were walking side by side, having a conversation about how much things cost. Two pounds, the Recruitment Consultant said, is too much. Way too much. You used to be able to get them for, what, one fifty at the most? The scurf narrowed, and they had to walk in single file for a short time. Then Alan spoke. I don't know, he said, I don't know. I don't think two pounds is that much. It is, though, it is, retorted the Recruitment Consultant. Both had pull-along suitcases that they pulled, with difficulty, along the roadside. The Recruitment Consultant was wearing a matching skirt and jacket that had cost, together, £69.99 and a blouse that had cost £19.99. Her shoes had cost £50, in the sale. The other items she wore came to no more than £10. I wouldn't, Alan said, pay more than two pounds, though. I've seen them for more, once I saw them for two fifty, I think, but that was in an airport. Mud was beginning to accumulate on their shoes. The backs of Alan's trousers were becoming

44

muddy. Alan and the Recruitment Consultant had known each other two weeks. I think, the Recruitment Consultant said, that two pounds is just too much. Alan said nothing, and they walked. The people in the cars that passed them were indistinct. Their cars were white, red, blue and black. Beyond the other side of the road were fields. On the other side of the hedgerow next to them was what they thought was the hotel. They were talking about how much things cost. The rain was not letting up. There's not much you can get, Alan said, for two pounds.

Alan and the Recruitment Consultant walked on, talking. They were searching for the turn-off that would lead to the hotel, but they were afraid they had gone too far and would have to turn back and find the road where they had been dropped off. They had seen no one else walking that they could ask directions of. The rain had begun to abate, but clouds the colour of fish in a shop hung above them. The hedgerow showed no signs of thinning out and the hotel was no longer visible through it. Cars went past. Ahead of them were road signs for the city they had driven from. I'm going to try to flag someone down, said the Recruitment Consultant, see if they can tell us where we are. Alan watched as the Recruitment Consultant stepped a little into the road, her arm waving. Nobody slowed down. Then there was a moment. Alan saw her slip, reached out to grab her but missed and saw her stumble into the road, get hit by a car, and fall and die with other cars skidding around her. The Recruitment Consultant died in the wet road. They never made the conference.

Sat in his chair, the bear dreams. It is this: I was sleeping, I often dream of sleeping, and I awoke, something woke me, in the dream. And I think it was the sound of a distant car alarm going off, the battery slowly wearing down, flattening the sound, stretching out the undulations of repetition. I sat up and listened for a small time, just a few seconds before the alarm stopped abruptly. The room was dark blue. I pulled the covers from around myself, stood up and stretched my arms out all the way to the finger tips. I padded to the kitchen to get some water, to look out the window. Pulling the curtain to one side I saw that everything was dark and still, like a game of musical statues. In the kitchen, I put a glass under the tap and switched it on. To my surprise, rather than water, out of the tap flowed hundreds of tiny white worms, the kind that might live in the anus. They flowed out of the tap and into my glass, which I dropped in surprise, but they continued to flow. Thousands of them, in great sticky, writhing globs, crawling in tiny caterpillar spasms, they began to fill up the sink, clogging the drain, sliding all over the slick walls, a mass of incoherent movement. Transfixed by this scene, I stood for a moment watching as more and more poured out of my tap. How could this be? They seemed less individuals, more a coherent entity. The sink gurgled with their slight noises. A thin detergenty film was sliding down the plughole as the first worms began to be crushed by the weight of the oncoming surge from the tap. Regaining my senses, I reached out, reluctantly, avoiding contact with the growing layer of worms at the bottom of my sink, and turned the tap, but it would not close tight. It just kept spinning loosely, and the worms kept pouring. I could not stop them now. Panicking, I backed out of the kitchen and returned to bed. Mark was still sleeping. This is all of the dream I remember, but I don't think it stopped there. The next morning I awoke tired and a little shaken. It was late, Mark had already left the house for work. I went down to the kitchen, pausing a little apprehensively before the door, but then chastising myself for the stupidity. As I opened the door, there was a slick sound I wasn't used to. For a moment I could not take the whole scene in: my writhing kitchen, tiny and like the picture on a fuzzy TV screen. The tap was still pouring out these tiny white worms – the dream was recurrent, or true – and my kitchen was full of these things. They had not made it quite as far as the door yet but they were over-flowing the sink now, which was full of a gluey white mass, still moving but mostly full of crushed dead worms. They spilled out over the surfaces, onto the washed-up plates and cutlery, out onto the floor a few of them, slowly filling the room. I could not make it to the tap now, could not get so far as to try to stem the flow. I felt dislocated from the scene and wondered where and how these worms had gotten into the pipes, whether this was happening to other people. I left the room and turned the TV on. There was nothing about it on the news. After the news I went back to the kitchen and they were still there, a few more of them now. They weren't coming out too fast but they weren't stopping either. I considered calling the police, but I didn't think I'd know what to say to them. I went out for a walk. I walked all the way into town, to Mark's office. I called in but they said he hadn't been in today. I think it concerned them that I didn't know where he was. I tried to call his mobile from a phonebox, but it went straight to voicemail. I . . . The bear's dream is interrupted. Louise is standing over him. Regis? Are you awake? I got your message, she says. How long have you been here? The bear looks up at her, his eyes gluey and red. He puts his claws into them. The tips sting his eyeballs. He cannot remember his dream. They are in the corridor of a hospital. How is she doing? Louise asks. The bear just looks at her forlornly. I'll get you a drink. Do you want coffee? She goes off to find a machine. Louise comes back a minute later and she sits down next to him. They sit silently. Time passes. There is the sense of time passing. You . . . Louise begins, but abandons the sentence. Louise looks at the window opposite them. Through the translucent glass she can just see indistinct shapes of light. Regis's mother is in there, she thinks, and she is dying. After a time a nurse comes along and lets them in. There is an old woman in the bed in the room. It appears that she is dying. She is so tiny, says Louise. The bear looks at her and then looks down at the woman on the bed. She is underneath a pink blanket. There are all kinds of tubes protruding from all kinds of places on her. The bear grips the bars at the side of the bed and leans heavily on them. A card on the bedside table depicts a unicorn leaping over a rainbow. There is a teddy bear beside it, a generic bear with a big gooey grin. It holds a plush red heart with the words GET WELL SOON! embroidered on it.

The Recruitment Consultant's manager called her into the office. She, the manager, was a tall woman. There had been a situation, a problem. It was to do with one of the temps. This temp had had a miscarriage and had been in hospital for a few days. She had phoned in and explained what was going on. When this was relayed to the manager at the company she worked for, he decided that it probably wouldn't be appropriate for her to continue working there. It was the Recruitment Consultant's job to relay this information back to the temp. This guy, who was her manager at the company, he didn't think that after such a stressful event, she would be able to handle the workload that would be expected of her. Really, he thought, it would be unfair on her to make her continue working in an environment that might upset her. The Recruitment Consultant asked if he would like to maybe discuss this with the temp, who might feel differently, but the manager said that it would be better coming from the agency, and he felt as though he was making the right decision with regard to her ability to continue in the job and, besides, she had already missed three days of work and would be likely to miss more in future. He needed someone more reliable than that. The Recruitment Consultant got off the phone and added the job to the board of available jobs and then scanned down her list of available people to try to find someone suitable. The job was a bit of filing, some basic admin work, answering the phone, stuff like that. There were plenty of available people and it was, really, pretty much arbitrary how she chose between them for a job like that. The problem really was what to say to the temp who had just been fired, the woman who had just had that miscarriage. It was a bit of a tricky one. This is why she had fed the details back to her manager, who was the manager of the whole of that branch of the recruitment agency. This manager had an irritating habit of wanting to hear every-thing twice, so she asked the Recruitment Consultant to explain what had happened, something the Recruitment Consultant had already done by email. What exactly is going on? she said. Well, said the Recruitment Consultant, what it is is that basically this woman was working as an admin assistant for Ultimate Storage Lords and on Monday she phoned in to say that she wasn't well. She phoned up later that day to say that she'd been in hospital and that she'd had a miscarriage. She didn't speak to me, she spoke to Tanya. Tanya called James, who's her line manager at Ultimate Storage Lords, but he was in a meeting at the time. Anyway this morning he phoned through and told us that he doesn't want her to work for them any more and that he wants a new temp by Monday if possible. Right, said the manager, OK. Well, I have to say I'm not happy about this. The last time I spoke to James Furlong he was having a go at us for not sending out invoices quickly enough and now he's coming back to us with an order and not coming through to me with it. I've told him time and time again that orders for a replacement have to come directly to me. He's not daft, he knows this. I've half a mind to ring him now. I've pulled him up for doing this before, more than once. And you know his manager, Julia? She's just as bad. She's had four PAs in six months and each time she hasn't put the order form in correctly. Next time when James Furlong does ring in with an order can you just put him straight through to me, please? The Recruitment Consultant furrowed her brow. OK, she said, normally I would have done, only you were in a meeting this morning. Not appearing to hear her, the manager continued, And another thing that James Furlong has said to me in the past is that our temps are less competent than ones he's got from other agencies! I sez to him, and you know this, she nodded at the Recruitment Consultant, that our tests are more rigorous than Capitol Secretarial's and Cheneric Recruitment's, and we come away with better feedback generally. And I don't know if you heard about what happened at Precision Bindings World? You know last week when Terry Andrews said he wasn't going to use us any more because too many temps had been walking out? Well, he went to Asterisk Appointments and four of their people walked out during the first morning! All four just went. Anyway he emailed me this morning asking if we could pick up the contract again. I've told him I'd have to think it over because I don't know if he's a reliable enough client. Haha, haha. Ha. The phone began to ring. The manager glanced up at the Recruitment Consultant. She answered the phone. Hello? . . . Oh, all right, Paula? . . . Yeah, not so bad. You'll never guess who I've had on the email this morning . . . Oh, he copied you in, did he? . . . Haha yeah! I've sent one back to him saying I'll have to think it over because I don't know if he's a reliable enough client! Haha, Ahaha. Ha. . . Yeah, well he'll think twice now before going somewhere else . . . I know. Well, at least the shit we send him last longer than two hours . . . Exactly . . . I might send him some of the dregs, just as punishment . . . haha, yeah . . . I might send him Carly McGuire . . . hahah. Haha! Can you imagine those two in an office together!? . . . You what? Oh, right, OK . . . no, I'm on flexi leave that day . . . Yeah, well, whenever. All right, see you later. She put the phone down. She looked up at the Recruitment Consultant, who looked back at her. Right, well, said the manager, like I say, I'm not happy about this. It's getting to the point where he's not showing us any respect. What I'll do is I'll ring him and have a word with him. The thing is, he doesn't seem to realise that ultimately this bad practice hurts him, not us, because I'll come down on him hard each time that he does it. It's not on really. She sat back. All right, well, she continued, I've got a meeting in Fieldhouse Street in half an hour so . . . She half-rose from her chair. Uh, the Recruitment Consultant interjected, I wanted to ask . . . The manager cut her off, Right, right. What did you want to ask? Her tone was aggressive now, harried. Well, said the Recruitment Consultant, What should I say to the woman who had the miscarriage? The manager slumped back down in her chair. Is she on the availability list? The Recruitment Consultant replied that she was, that she was willing to come back to work as soon as Monday as she needed the money, but that she still thought she would be working for Ultimate Storage Lords. Well, said the manager, I wouldn't really have her as a high priority. What sort of work is it that she's looking for? The

Recruitment Consultant replied that she was looking for basic admin work. Well, the manager sighed, you can put her on the list but I wouldn't put her as a high priority. People have to understand that they can't take days off and then go swanning back into work the following Monday as if nothing's happened. I think, in fact, we're going to have to crack down on this sort of thing. It's happening too much and managers don't like it. We have to take a harder line on people taking days off. But, the Recruitment Consultant said, she was in hospital, she was having a miscarriage. Surely we . . . The manager cut her off again. I'm not talking about specific cases, I'm talking about in general. In general we have to take a harder line and say to these people, if you're not going to work your contracted hours then I'm not sure you can continue to work with us. Could you feed that back to the others, please? I've really got to get to this meeting now. The manager got up, grabbed her coat and left the room. The Recruitment Consultant sat thoughtfully in her chair. She felt a little nauseous. She stood up and the nausea increased. Her eyes clouded over and she could only see an orange and black field with little blue spots meandering across it. She blinked her eyes repeatedly but they would not clear. She groped around for something to steady herself but her hands only seemed to knock things to the floor. She heard something clatter and then must have stumbled over it because she tripped and fell and was dead when she hit the floor.

Simon is in a taxi with the bear and Gill, who is just some woman. They are on the way back from a party. They have been drinking. The taxi driver is playing a talk radio station. In my opinion – this is just my opinion, feel free to disagree with this, the host is saying – women should not be allowed to drink alcohol. He pauses for a long time. Think about it. What looks more disgusting than a drunk woman? Think about it. Why do men get drunk? Why do they do it? They do it to impress women. They do it to give them confidence when they're out on the pull. Women . . . if women didn't drink it would stop fights outside clubs on a Friday night. What are most of the fights you see about? I'd say nine out of ten fights, I'd say maybe ninety-nine out of one hundred fights between blokes are over some girl. If we stopped women drinking, I'm telling you, ninety-nine out of one hundred of those fights would be prevented. Hey, hey, Simon goes, change the station, man. Put something techno on. Put some house on. Simon has been talking about house music all night. Simon has a can of lager in his hand. In his other hand he has a bucket of takeaway chicken. Hold this, Simon says, passing the can to Gill, who is sitting in between Simon and the bear. He takes some chicken out of the bucket and puts it into his mouth. Simon's eyes roll back in his head. He sits back and chews on the chicken. His mouth is all greasy. That chicken is so greasy. Simon is so high, he can barely talk. He can barely sit still. It's a feeling, says Simon, house is a feeling. The bear looks out of the window. They are passing a place that sells used cars. There are tinsel streamers in red, blue and silver strung out across the whole place, from the roof of the office to the top of the signs. Behind, flats loom up. They drive. Simon and the girl are kissing now. Simon has his hand inside her top. They have chicken grease all around their mouths. Simon pushes her back into the seat. He rears away. He is looking at the chicken. He picks up a leg. Do you want some? Uh, do you want some of this chicken, man? He is looking at the bear. You can have some of my chicken . . . if you want. The bear shakes his head sadly. Here, look. Can you hold this? Simon lets the bucket drop from his hand. Chicken bones are all on the floor of the taxi. The bear leans down and picks up the bucket, which is nearly empty, only pieces of brown fried skin and grease clinging to the bottom. Simon is pulling the girl's skirt up. She is laughing, just laughing with all that grease around her mouth, her lipstick smeared in splodges. She wipes around her chin with the palm of her hand and runs the hand up over her face and through her hair. She can't stop laughing. Simon pulls her knickers down over her knees. He has a piece of the chicken in his hand, a chicken leg, and he stops to take a bite. He says something incomprehensible with his mouth stuffed with chicken. They both laugh. The bear coughs. Simon puts his head between the girl's legs, starts licking her thighs, her clitoris. She laughs more. She puts her hands in his hair and tilts her head back, her eyes closed, laughing and laughing. The grease all over her legs and stomach dimly reflects the orange light as they pass. The voice on the radio goes, People in council houses shouldn't be allowed to smoke. Think about it. Do those people own their houses? Well, obviously they don't, the council owns them. Those houses are council property. What happens when you smoke in a house? What happens?! The walls turn yellow, it smells nasty, it ruins the furniture. The value of the house is going to go down if a smoker is living there. The house deteriorates. And what's with people in council houses smoking anyway? If you can't afford a house what are you doing wasting money on cigarettes! It's ridiculous. Simon crunches into bone with his teeth. He is leaning across the girl, his head between her legs. Now he lurches back, his hand to his mouth. Shit. He throws the bone down on the floor. He looks across at the bear. Have you eaten all that chicken?

As soon as the bear entered the world, there was work. To be human, it seemed, there had to be work. To have the things that defined people, you had to have the money to afford them, and to have that, you had to work. Similarly, work itself defined people. When he found work, the bear was surprised at how much time it took up. Though less complex, his society among other bears had not been founded on the principle of work – when they had enough to eat, when they had done what was necessary, they stopped and were leisurely.

Working in an office, he could finish all the necessary tasks and then ask his manager what to do. The manager, always hassled, always put upon, would sigh at the bear. He had been working too fast again. Then he or she would find some filing for the bear to do, or some tidying up, or something. Alternatively, there would be nothing to do, but even in those situations the bear was not free to leave the office. He had to sit there and look at the screen of his computer, look busy.

The bear could not comprehend fully the logic of this and it got him down. It seemed as though work was not so much something that you did, as a place you went to and stayed at for a set period of time, whether there was anything to do or not. It was rarely made clear to the bear, as he went from temp job to temp job, exactly who he was working for, or who he was making money for, or how his filing or data entry fitted into a larger schema. There was never time for the managers to explain that. Or perhaps they too were unaware. On the bus in the mornings, the bear could see the dark pull that work exerted on the shrunk-pink faces that rode with him.

He was tired, but tiredness was the true state of work; fatigue could not be stretched out of limbs, lassitude could not be pushed aside. In a variety of offices, the bear spent idle moments conceiving of his role in the structure of that organisation. From his understanding, it rarely seemed as though what he was meaningful. Mostly it was tasks too boring for middle managers or secretaries, handed down and down until they were so undesired that only agency staff would do them. Agency staff were expendable and the tasks they performed so simple and mundane that, though they frequently left, they were easily replaced. It was logical that if you have only an hour and a half of data entry to stretch over a seven-hour day, then your rate of pay would be low. What was not logical was to express dissatisfaction with the state of things. To prick the silent bubble of work was a terrible thing to do. If the bear said to the staff at the agency he was employed by that he didn't have enough work to do they would chastise him, tell him to talk to his line manager. There would always be, in the tone of their voices, the implication that he was stupid or naïve for revealing the flaws in his job. Don't you want to work?

If such minor quibbles caused consternation, to question the open secret of work was far worse. If the bear asked his employment agency how much per hour they were paid while he worked, or if he asked what exactly he was doing, or who he was doing it for, if he questioned the naturalness of the situation, intimated that there was something amiss, then he would be met with the sudden change in countenance characteristic of Recruitment Consultants. Their faces would drop and all the friendliness formerly in their tone would change to aggression and defensiveness.

To ask about details was fine, to ask about what kind of chair you would sit in, what kind of clothes you were permitted to wear, how big the office was. Those things were fine. What wasn't fine was to ask exactly what the company did, or how the recruitment process worked. It wasn't fine to ask what you could do when you'd finished the work you were given and there wasn't any more to do. It wasn't fine to point out the sexism of managers, nor their racism, nor their homophobia. It wasn't fine to question the legitimacy or validity of the work you were doing, nor to express concern over the ethical status of the company you were working for.

The one power a temp has is to leave. The bear, several times, left a job in the middle of the day. During lunch he would make the decision not to go back or he would just get up and leave. It felt so great. It felt great to have leisure, the bear almost thought that he was stealing that leisure. The one protest a temp can make is to quit. They make this protest knowing that it will only really affect them. The company will have someone else by Monday.

Quitting is always a pyrrhic victory for the temporary worker. If you quit, regardless of the reason, it's unlikely that your agency will find you work again, and there are a finite number of agencies in each town. Competence, intelligence, willingness to learn are all irrelevant to the agency. What they desire is reliability: someone who will turn up every day, not get sick, not ask questions.

The problem for the bear is that he cannot simply return to the woods if no longer satisfied with life among humans. He cannot simply quit. To be human is to acquire debt. And debt must be paid back, and debt accumulates. Unless you are one of the fortunate few hundred in the world to whom debt is paid, then you must pay it. To abscond is not conceivable. Were the bear to let his fur grow back and return, naked to his brethren, he would be chased down and made to pay. He would be put back into work. To live in the world is to owe something. If the bear had known this, would he have made the same decisions?

The farmer leaves his house. Skin cracked from cold, head like egg. It is morning but there is no sun, the sky and sea the colour of dry pavement and dusty glass. The line of the horizon barely, just barely, distinguishable. He is wrapped in coats, big and brown. His coat has five pockets, but just one, the secret one hidden inside the coat, under his arm, against his heart, is full. He feels the front of the coat, against where the pocket is, with a gloved hand and marks out the hard shape, something like a tooth, longer though, perhaps less hard. But it is his song, his music. The sand is pitch and in front of him it stretches, grey, night grey, deep in its desolation. Behind him are the marshes, dangerous damplands. He looks ahead, toward the arcs of brown rock, where the cliff meets the sea and the beach curls to its own drab end. He walks along the scurf, the sand heavy beneath him, damp, difficult to penetrate. The tide, coming in; on its way in, the greying water flicks his dark shoes, edges away his footprints. His heelmarks that fill with water, that fill with green water and break up, the outlines softening, turning less hard, filling with grey water and foam, effacing. He looks ahead of him, brown scarf bunched around his chin, moist where he blows out into it. In the sand around him the farmer sees empty beer bottles, the shrivelled remains of crisp packets, chip cartons, cans and cans of Coke. To his left are the dunes, shingle escarpments rough with thick waxy grass and arduous pathways stubbed with glass. A friend of the bear's has been going on for ages about visiting the zoo, so one weekend he agrees to accompany her. The bear hulks along among the cages. It's cruel, don't you think, to see them cooped up like this? They look so sad, says Lisa. They are looking at a cage with a leopard in it. The leopard is asleep in one corner. She turns and looks at him and the bear looks back at her. Something passes between them. She turns away and begins to walk towards the giraffe enclosure. The giraffe is standing and looking pensively at the trees on the hill above the zoo. The bear, too, stands and looks at the trees. He begins to follow her. She has stopped in front of the giraffe. This is fun, she says, turning to the bear. The bear looks at the giraffe, which continues to look at the trees. It is cold. The giraffe looks like it has patches of rust on it. It is dirty, it is fat, its teeth are horrible. Its legs looks spindly, it does not seem to understand its captivity, it continues to strain its neck while it looks over at some trees. Being winter, the trees on the ridge are just bare branches. The enclosure is four brown walls, a brown floor and brown hay in a corner. There are pools of brown water on the concrete and piles of black giraffe pellets in the pools. This giraffe is called Terry, he was born in the zoo and is now fully grown, Lisa reads from a sign on the wall.

Inside the reptile house, with the bright staring eyes of frogs and the lethargy of the snakes, the bear gets too hot, has to leave and sit down outside. His breath, big in the air, comes in grey plumes. Are you all right? Lisa puts the back of her hand on the bear's forehead, on skin that feels scrubbed hard and is pink. The bear looks up at her. He puts his hands on his knees and pulls himself up with effort. He looks down at her.

When they see the spiders, especially the tiny brilliant black widow, which is moving, the bear grows jumpy and agitated. He begins to scratch his skin all the time, feeling constant itches and the presence of insects. Out of the corners of his eyes he is sure he keeps spying movements.

They go to the penguin enclosure. It is noisy there, there are quite a few families. I've never liked penguins, says Lisa, I've always found them bizarre. There's something weird about them. I don't know, I think I associate them with death. Isn't that weird? Animals in general I've always associated with death. Penguins in particular but animals in general, I guess. I suppose it's the way they approach death, you know. They don't think about it. They spend their whole lives avoiding it, but just by instinct. It's only because that's all they know that they don't just die straight away. But then in some ways, we're the same. I mean people. We know just enough to think about it, but we still act the same, we don't know enough to rise above that. I've always been sad that people aren't smarter, you know. Like when you see films on the TV or read a book about an alien civilisation and they're always so civilised and advanced and intelligent. It seems like we have the worst luck really. We're too clever not to be aware of what we are, but not clever enough to live together properly. She looks up at the bear. Just then, a kid drops a toy, a die-cast metal car, into the enclosure. The penguins cluck and shriek and jump back towards the corner. Lisa makes a face. I don't like penguins. Can we go? she says.

The Recruitment Consultant's full name was Carol Rebecca Trevelyan, but she had many other names. Her maternal grandparents always called her Carol, just that. She had never liked her first name and had insisted on being called Rebecca at school, which her friends shortened to Becky, Becca or Bec. Her parents both called her Rebecca, always the full name. At work a man called Steve, after finding out her surname, found it funny to call her Trev or Trevor, and that was sometimes adopted by some of her other colleagues, but mostly these days, at work and elsewhere she was Carol or, to some clients, Miss Trevelyan. Her boyfriend, Richard, called her, for obscure reasons, Gary, Gaz or Gazza. Sometimes in moments of seriousness he would look at her and call her Carol and that made her feel OK.

The bear steps from the hot of the street into the cool of the cinema foyer. It is a Tuesday. He drops his eyes as he gives the cash to the girl behind the counter. He doesn't feel well. Lately the terrible headaches that begin behind his right eyeball have returned, and today bubbles of sick-tasting gas keep rising in his throat and bursting in his mouth. It tastes of sick, the world, today. He takes his change. He forces his eyes to meet the girl's and gives a weak grin. She smiles back. He lingers around, there are some minutes still before the film starts. At the next desk he buys a Coke, and as he walks through a set of swinging double doors, the roar of the bubbles in the Coke seems so loud in the sudden silence that it overcomes him for a moment. And he stands, even in this moment of anxiety and confusion, making sure he appears to be looking at a poster of a girl with a headscarf and a title he can't read. The gas of sick in his mouth, the bubbles in his ears, he waits it out. It passes. He walks over to the toilets, enters the stall, pours a good third of the Coke into the bowl, opens his bag and replaces the difference from a bottle of vodka.

The theatre is cooler still, and he takes a seat towards the back, in the middle. The place is practically empty. It is the middle of the day. The trailers play and the bear pays attention. The gas in the Coke rises back up his throat with a new sheen of vomit taste after every sip, but he drinks, nonetheless, trying to float the taste out of the side of his open mouth, or curl up his tongue as he feels it rise.

The film begins with a shot of a room at dusk, with crumbling plaster but a still regal air to the faded furniture. A country house. An old record, maybe Django Rheinhardt, plays over the still shot. The air is dim outside the window, and orange, and fading, a hint of the sea or the countryside in the dip of the silhouetted land. The music, stiff guitar and trumpet drenched in crackles, seems to decay further as it plays on until the notes are submerged in distortion and the sound becomes a warped seascape and the bear realises slowly that it is a treated record, or a pastiche. And the camera, too, begins slowly to pan away from the house, which isn't a house at all, but the ruined facade of one, with half a faded sofa, cut right through the middle cushion and nothing beyond. And destroyed walls around the window, which gives onto a cliff and a road and the sea. And on the road is a drab figure, a woman. And that, it is clear, is the start of the film.

It is shot in the 'cold' style of a seventies TV series, and in mostly natural light. The characters are blankness/sadness/dread.

The film follows the actions of five characters who live in the destroyed house of the opening shot. Only it isn't destroyed when they lived there. They destroy it, in a fire. The fire comes at the end of the film.

The farmer is a character with a green hat. He has side-burns. He carries a stick. It seems that farming was merely an affectation for him, a mode of expression, a style of dress. In one pivotal scene he is talking with the philosopher, another character. They meet in the park. The farmer is explaining how he is thinking about getting this little patch of land just outside the city. How he'd gone down there and stayed for a few days. How there was enough space for some livestock, good grazing for cows and sheep, good soil for vegetables. He is going to go all organic, the farmer says, go for the new markets. He asks the philosopher if he wants in on it: half the profits, a place to stay, a share of the produce, half of everything. The farmer puffs out his chest, his eyes glinting, and says, There's a time in the morning, around sunrise, at the top of the hill behind the new house, you can see the whole city stretching out in the valley below. And the view is different every day. It depends on the weather, on the sun, on the clouds. He stands there proudly looking at the philosopher, whose eyes are to the ground. The philosopher doesn't even seem to think. The philosopher looks up at him, You cunt, he shouts. He just keeps shouting, You stupid cunt. You stupid cunt.

The invalid is the only woman of the group. It is her that you could see in the opening shot of the film, walking down the road, side-on to the camera. There is a very long scene in the film where she paints a crude walrus with acrylics. The walrus's body is blue. His background is pink.

They put on a pantomime. They hold it in the garden of their house. The philosopher and the clown play the pan-tomime horse. The clown is the front end and the philoso-pher is the back end. Wait, wait, is it the other way around? They cut the head from the horse costume and replace it with the real head of the dead pig which the philosopher wears. The pig is wearing those novelty googly-eyed glasses with eyeballs on the ends of slinky springs. The DJ pro-vides the music for the pantomime. It is mainly astral jazz, fusion, Balearic, Bollywood soundtracks, that sort of thing.

The invalid is doing a mural of great British fascists. Her Wyndham Lewis looks disappointingly blithe. Her Oswald Mosley bears a striking resemblance to David Seaman. Her William Joyce has hands much larger than his head. As she draws and draws with a charcoal stick, the other four stand behind her, weeping sombrely. She starts on her Nick Griffin. He is holding a sword and his hands are black. He is looking up to the sky, biting his lip. The resemblance is devastatingly striking.

These events culminate in the poignant end sequence of the film in which their house burns down and one of the group, caught in the flames, dies. What happens is this: the invalid is finishing off her mural, adding a phalanx of horses, storming across a misty plain, to one corner, when her stick of charcoal breaks. She puts her cigarette down and goes to find another box. The DJ in the room above turns the bass on his boombox up; he is playing one of his favourite tapes. The vibrations from the music dislodge the cigarette, which rolls and falls among the philosopher's many tracts and pamphlets, which are stacked against the wall. Dry and dusty as they are, they catch instantly and soon the whole room is ablaze. While the farmer, the invalid, the philosopher and the DJ make their way out of the house, the clown, playing around inside the back end of the horse costume, frolics unaware. The blaze grows and grows. The camera pans back to show the whole house consumed by the conflagration and then moves slowly across the four faces, illuminated orange with flame. It is raining outside. The philosopher (or is it the clown?) and the DJ are talking with their heads down. The invalid has salvaged a box of trinkets from her bedroom and is looking wistfully at it. The farmer isn't looking at the house; the audience see him in profile. He is looking past the house, at the sea below.

◆

The shot pulls back to show all four of them silhouetted against the house. Bright flames lick the top of the screen. In full surround-sound the bear hears the crackles and snares of the fire as it grows and consumes. A dirge begins to play. Some trumpet comes from the back of the cinema and moves forward, obscuring the noise of the fire. It is 'St James Infirmary'; the bear recognises it as that. The first solo ends and a man begins to sing, coarse and deep. The camera moves up, over the house, over the town, through the sky, which is growing dark and translucent. As the vocal line is completed and the solo starts up again, the bear, impossibly moved, rises from his seat and bursts into applause, tears in his eyes. All eyes in the cinema train on him. The screen goes black. The credits begin to roll.

Suddenly self-conscious, the bear runs a hand through his hair, looks around him, and quickly leaves the cinema. Out on the pavement the heat blasts him and he feels sick, sick again.

The DJ was walking home. He had been walking pretty much the whole day with his earphones in and techno, always techno, was what was in them. Only now that his battery was getting lower was he walking back up the hill towards his house. Techno. It was always techno for him. Techno, he liked to say, was his connection to the cosmos. If you asked the DJ what he thought about techno he would tell you that the heavens moved at one hundred and twenty five bpm. He would tell you that techno is everything that is potential, and it is everything that is cyclical, and it is everything that is mystical, and it is everything that is ritualistic. Techno is a religion and also an atheism. Techno is a Zen, it is a Tao, it is a mantra, it is a sutra. It's a litany about everything and nothing in the transcendent. Techno tells people about things. It tells people all about themselves, all about their place in nature. Techno shows us that words are less than everything. Techno is what is outside the text. Techno is beyond the end of history. Techno. Techno. Techno. Techno. Techno is as empty as anything else. Techno looks back at the panopticon and gives it the finger. Techno is an incredulity towards meta-musics. Techno. Techno is the cultural logic of late nights. Techno is finding the key to the cage but refusing to break yourself out. Techno is just music. Dare to techno. Techno deals with the two crucial unexplored paradises: space and under the sea. These are just some of the things that the DJ would tell you about techno. For him, for the DJ, techno was a state of being, a methodology of thinking. For him socialism was a kind of techno (the right wing, of course, lack the rhythmic quality to be regarded as techno).

The battery was getting lower and the light was fading. With his thick tongue and his dry skin, the DJ ascended. His house was where he lived and he lived with a couple of other guys. He lived with the farmer and with the clown, he lived with the invalid and the philosopher. These were the guys he lived with and, though they did not have too deep an understanding of techno, he still liked to live with them. They were OK.

Of that crowd, the philosopher was probably the most interesting. Or was it the clown? Once, he made a finger puppet of Kant and another of Deleuze and he did a little puppet show for the others of what would have happened if they had ever met in real life. It was funny because when he did it Kant spoke a bit like a surfer, which he probably did not ever do when he was really alive, and Deleuze spoke with this real cut-glass accent. That was funny. What was good about the show was that it illuminated various aspects of the debate between philosophers like Deleuze and neo-Kantian philosophers like finger-puppet Kant. Every time he read an article about the financial crisis, the philosopher would just laugh and laugh. He started calling himself a Marxist and cut out pictures from the newspaper of failing banks and distressed-looking stockbrokers. The clown told him that he could understand the schadenfreude, but it would be the poor people that suffered in the end. It will be us poor that end up suffering for this. They began to shout at each other and, because the DJ had turned up the volume on this huge new remix he had just bought, it was really hard to tell, in the final analysis, who was shouting what. Neither of them felt that poor people suffering was a good thing. Because why would they?

The farmer was in the shop but he was only buying some biscuits. You can't farm biscuits, so that's why he had to buy them. You can farm some of the ingredients though. He had these biscuits that were cheaply packaged, cheaply made and they tasted cheap too. They were just one plain layer of biscuit – no filling or no chocolate. The farmer could afford more expensive biscuits, he was not a thrifty man by any means. He had even tasted more expensive biscuits. But he liked these cheap biscuits best of all. People mostly looked at the farmer like he was a piece of shit. Like there was something grotesque about his wax jacket and wellington boots. He did look out of place in their town, but that was no reason for the looks he got. People would just stare at his sideburns. He got to the till and the girl there scanned his packet of biscuits, trying not to touch the packet where the farmer's hands had been. She looked at him and she looked nauseous. She said an amount of money. The farmer reached into his trouser pockets and pulled out a handful of coins covered in flakes of dry grey tissues and the honest dirt of the earth, the land that he loved to till. He handed over the coins indiscriminately, not even counting them. The girl looked like he had just put so much muck in her hands. She gave him way too much change, so the biscuits turned out to be even cheaper.

The farmer walked along the road back towards his house, whistling a bright tune. Doo doo doo, doo doo doo doo. He opened the packet and ate a biscuit. The season was getting colder and the earth would be harder in the mornings, it would not yield so easily. Still, still, he liked to go out early and stamp hard on the frosty grass and hear the sound it made and feel the cold in his feet and see his boots damp with dew and watch his breath make curlicues in the air. By now the streetlights were on all the way up his hill and in the distance faintly the farmer could see the blocks of green and red light coming out of the DJ's room. If he removed his hat and strained his ears he could hear, carried on the slight breeze, the faintest propulsion, the tenderest beat.

The Recruitment Consultant struggled up the hill. It was getting cold, but she didn't want to go any faster up the hill because her neighbour, the one who resembled a farmer, was on the other side of the street and a lot of times he would smile at her in a creepy way and other times he would even speak to her in an accent that was inexplicably simultaneously Cornish and Welsh. Also she could already hear that fucking guy's trance music from over the road. She was going to have to say something to the council about that. It was getting beyond a joke. She took a sip from her can. She had bought eight cans of lager.

The invalid had been stuck in her bed all day, sick. It had

been another tough day. She had spent most of the day doing preliminary sketches for a new mural she was planning. The plan so far was for it to be of right-wing figures who had come out in support of Barack Obama – the central panel was going to be Tom Metzger and Colin Powell locked in an intense arm wrestle, but with their faces in dead hard smiles. These two figures would be far larger and far more detailed than any of the others in the mural. The question you as a spectator would have to ask would be are they happy or are they compromised? And to what extent am I, the spectator, myself compromised by the very act of representation? The invalid would argue that you are always compromised, you are always implicit in whatever politics you encounter in art. She would sit up in her bed and take down a long clear quartz crystal and say that just as a part of you is lost to the crystal whenever you touch it, so a part of you is lost to any artwork you encounter. The other part of her mural would be portraits of so-called left-wing politicians who supported the Iraq war. In the mural they would be dressed in dirty Gulf War soldier uniforms and would have wounds on their faces and black blindfolds over their eyes. Yes, yes, she would say, it was a political artwork. But it was one that was ambivalent about the possibility of a real future politics separate from a bland centrist discourse governed principally by secret cabal-nexuses of corporate power. The issue, of course, was political representation versus artistic representation. When she was planning a mural or a painting, as she frequently was, the others in the house tended to stay away from the invalid. She was very boring on the subject of her art and it was hard to continue to be encouraging when, as they all knew, her paintings always failed. In the sketches she had been making, Colin Powell looked like he was cocking a snook at a Tom Metzger who looked like he was flexing one enormous set of biceps.

At one stage in the day, the clown had brought her a sandwich. She had been working on a sketch of the upper left-hand corner, which was to be taken up by the left-wing Iraq apologists, and had started to explain in detail the symbolic resonance of some of their gestures: Well . . . hm. It kind of symbolises a kind of. Well, it's a kind of . . . hm. It's not really about . . . Well, hm. It's kind of . . . not really about politics today. It's more. Well. It's more like it's about politics . . . I mean, well, it is political but it's like. It's about the politics of, hm . . . the past but . . . looking towards the, hm, you know, the near future . . . but it's that but it's represented by. Well. It's kind of. They are not exactly represented . . . but, you know, represented? They are kind of represented by the figures in the painting. All the clown could see in the piece of paper he had been given were some stick men with black lines across their totally round heads. You know, said the clown, gesturing with his piece of paper at the scattered drawings on and around the bed, These people, they all suffered, they struggled. Whatever they did, they did it suffering. None of them escaped that. The invalid looked back at him with her fat face a contorted mask of confusion. She seemed spent. This isn't, she said, looking at her drawings, I mean . . . it's . . . I don't think these are that. She said that with a sigh. I don't think, she

continued, I mean . . . it's not. It's not that. I don't think . . .
I don't think it's really, you know . . . that.

Just as she got through her door, the Recruitment Consultant's phone tinkled. What a pleasing noise! The message
said something like Where R U? or at least it had that
general gist. She held the phone in front of her for a while,
wondering what to do with it. She needed to sit down and
so she did. She sat on the sofa in her living room and the
phone fell away from her free hand. She put the cans up
on the table. The idea of drinking them seemed in some
ways good and in other ways bad. Likewise, the idea of not
drinking them, in some ways it seemed good and in other
ways it seemed bad. The best solution seemed to be to start
or continue drinking them, whichever, and see how it went.

The clown was easily the most interesting of that crowd.
Wait. No. It could be the philosopher. The clown was an
amusing kind of guy. He was a joker. He was forever telling
jokes and playing practical jokes. He would tell endless
variations on his favourite joke. The joke had a particular
structure, within which infinite deviations were possible.
The punchline of the joke was always 'You don't understand, x is the name of my dog!' where x is the main vari-
ational phrase in the joke. For example: A man walks into
a bar and orders a beer. He looks pensive, so the barman
asks him if anything is wrong. Well, replies the man, Last
night I got drunk and accidentally had sex with my wife's
sister and her daughter. The barman laughs. Well, sport,
he says, What your wife doesn't know won't hurt her, right?

You don't understand, the man replies, my wife's sister and her daughter is the name of my dog!

She left the bread toasting under the grill and, can in hand, made her way up the stairs. Downstairs her phone was ringing, but she could no longer hear it, was oblivious to it. Her bedroom looked like shit. It had not been tidied for days. She noticed a book on the floor, spine cracked open. The book was overdue at the library. I must phone the library about that! she said out loud, and started to turn back towards the stairs. But then, realising there were more important things, she sipped from her can and, using the door frame for support, turned back into the room. She stepped over clothes and junk until she reached the wardrobe. She opened the wardrobe. Downstairs, the bread was blackening. She pulled out the suit and put it down on the bed. Faintly, she could discern the DJ's music coming from the house across the road, but it no longer bothered her. She removed her clothes. She held the suit up and stepped into it. With some difficulty she zipped it up. She walked to the mirror and looked into it. All around her reflection was the detritus of her regular existence, the dust and shame of it. The ugly clothes she regularly wore, the tragic imprint of her voice, everything she said which never reflected her real feelings, her bad skin, the terrible catch in her voice when she nervously spoke too quickly. All these things faded from her consciousness now, though, as she looked at her reflected self in the bear suit in the mirror. A bear is uncompromisingly strong, silent, stoical. A bear is primal, animalistic, without language. A bear is noble, beyond politics, beyond the petty vagaries of human interaction. A bear.

The DJ was pitching this one record up so that the beat would syncopate with this other record he had of Alan Watts talking about Zen. His set had started off with just this like ambient rumble, slowly gaining momentum before he dropped this huge breakdown totally unexpectedly before he dropped the bpm to blend the beat with this dancehall track. Now he mixed in this modern classical record that sounded like thousands of insects all chattering to each other and slowly faded the beat out so that it was just Watts talking over the metallic clang of the insects. He was so busy adding an echo effect to Watts' voice, then a robotic-sounding effect, then another filter so that rather than speech it began to sound like the ghost of speech, just spattering and whirring along, he was so busy cueing up this great motorik beat and fading it in, that he failed to hear the Recruitment Consultant's cooker explode in the house opposite. It wasn't until the crackle from the fire failed to beatmatch with this great early Chicago house track that he'd just downloaded that he looked up from his setup (two turntables, two CDJs, two laptops and a cross-fader) and saw that the whole of the downstairs was ablaze. He pressed pause on the laptop and took his headphones off. He took time to note that this would be a good point in the set to drop that 2pac a cappella before running down-stairs.

Lying back on her bed, the Recruitment Consultant thought

of forests. She thought of wet grass. With her eyes closed she pictured frothing streams of clear water, running in narrow channels over green rocks, swarming with fish. Rapt, she transformed her shrill voice into a low growl. She growled and growled, as loud as she could muster. Then, swigging again from another can, she thought of bright green leaves, flecked with early autumnal yellow, wavering in the wind. Of fields of flowers and bulrushes along the riverbank. She thought of birds. And she herself, as a bear, out in all that nature. Out with an instinct older than humanity, a knowledge of the world darker and more ancient than can be expressed in any language, but one that starkly animates each life. Though humans have long ago cast this knowledge aside, the Recruitment Consultant felt it flowing through her animal self, spurring her on to nobler, to more profound visions.

All of them except the DJ were in their kitchen. The philosopher was telling a little story. I was in a seminar the other day, he said. We were discussing Foucault and the emergence of phallogocentricism in the western conception and the tutor asked me whether it was possible to pinpoint an exact time in history when we could say this conception emerged and I said, Well, the western conception of phallogocentricism emerged from behind a tree, cocked his little leg and did a piss. The tutor looked shocked and asked me what the hell I was talking about. You don't understand, I replied. My dear instructor, you simply do not understand! The western conception of phallogocentricism is the name of my dog!

As the conflagration downstairs began to spread from the kitchen into the living room, the Recruitment Consultant thought of fields. The stink of herself is still on the bed, tangible in the slight mattress indentation and crumpled heap of sheets. She paces the room in the muggy light from the window. Outside there is a storm. She looks outside to see the landscape changing. Houses crack and dissolve in front of her, lightning bursts open a dead black tree. The sky shivers and she feels serene, limitless. She begins to remember in glorious detail the weft of her life, memories tinctured and happy, everyone smiling, everything right. In her mind connections form across the span of her recollections, she comes to see the motives of people who have wronged her and forgives them, comes to understand fully the stresses her parents faced, the cruelty of friends, and she forgives them in a moment of ecstatic benevolence. All around her, thunder claps and funereal music, drenching blissful chords, a glorious elemental drone plays and plays, syncopated by the noise of the thunder and the rain clacking against the house. Inside her arms and legs, in her groin, down her fingers the Recruitment Consultant feels a surge of clean bliss. Without malice the events of her life stand before her, bathed in colour, like watching the TV with the colour turned up, all the streets she's ever walked down clean and white. The land outside changes. In the distance mountains rise up, pierce through the clouds with serene trajectories, distant majesty. Far away buildings evaporate and people meld in a fiery coalescence which is

beautiful and silent, forest and jungle rise up where once
there were cities, the clocks all stop, the glaciers burn
up and become steam, the sea swells and runs and runs,
engulfing all the land but for one small portion. There was
nothing ugly or refined about what came. The Recruitment
Consultant's mind swells and she seems to begin to think in
a new, unheard-of language. Still the music plays on like a
vast edifice of plangent moans. Rain drenches the remaining land and the new plants slurp it up. She remembers
books that she has never read and the music sounds like
choirs and celestial waves. The room hums and shakes and
finally tips, the walls crack and crumble and the Recruitment Consultant falls without pain and lands asleep on
fresh wet grass.

The farmer stood with the others out on their lawn, watching the Recruitment Consultant's house burn down. He
leant heavily on his stick, feeling older. Rain had begun to
fall and a pair of dogs were chasing each other up and down
the street, alarmed and aggressive. The fire smacked and
howled; scornful and menacing it reared up over them. He
turned to the clown and said, Fire is always an anti-Catho-
lic symbol. It's a bad omen, this fire. He took the packet of
biscuits from his pocket and offered it around. You're right,
said the clown. You know, he continued, Just the other day
I was speaking to a guy and he told me that he'd accidentally set fire to a Catholic church with the whole congregation inside. That's terrible! the farmer exclaimed. It is!
replied the clown, But this guy didn't seem to be that upset
by it. I asked him why he was grinning at the recollection

(which he was) and he said to me, You don't understand, a Catholic church with the whole congregation inside is the name of my dog!

The dogs had all retreated to their houses. Behind the burning house, the gloaming was visible. The fire engines had arrived and firemen in their fluorescent outfits were pointing hoses at the house. In vain. The rain had got heavier and the wind had picked up. All the windows in the house had been broken and the fire sought more to consume. Before it burned her, the fire burned through the Recruitment Consultant's bear costume until nothing of it remained. She would have preferred it that way. If you could stand in her room, among the fire, and look out past the smoky shards of broken glass, you would see her neighbours, their faces picked out in flickering orange highlights, buffeted by the wind, wet from the rain, standing on the pavement looking back in at you.

The invalid was out with her sketchpad, taking down some ideas. Fire was particularly hard to draw. She hadn't realised that. She went back inside and returned with her camera, but the rain kept getting on her lens, and the blue light from the fire engines was ruining the composition. She turned to the philosopher (or was it the clown? It was hard to tell in this light) and said, I . . . you know. Hm. This reminds me of . . . no. It's not that . . . Well. You know that thing that. Wait, no. O. No, wait. I . . . yes. That thing that Stockhausen . . . wait? Was it Stockhausen? The philosopher rubbed his eyes and interjected, You are perhaps referring to Stockhausen's claim that the World Trade Center attacks were the greatest work of art? I . . . the invalid began to reply, Yes . . . I. Well, the philosopher interjected once more, it's funny you should mention that because I met with ol' Karlheinz a few weeks before his death and I spoke with him about it. Wasn't that an awful thing to say? I asked. Why, my dear boy, Stockhausen replied, you simply don't understand it at all! The World Trade Center attacks is the name of my dog!

It was mid-morning by the time the fire was finally out. The firefighters had been able to prevent the blaze from spreading to neighbouring houses (the Recruitment Consultant's house was semi-detached and the wind was in their favour), but everything she had owned had been destroyed. Walking through the sodden, blackened rooms, everywhere there were skeletons and filthy remnants of things. There were unreadable books with blackened pages, grown fat from all the water, like they had been dropped in the bath. There were photo frames, the pictures burnt up, but the cracked grey opaque glass remaining. When someone dies, a world dies. At the top of the stairs, still lying back on the remains of her bed, was the Recruitment Consultant's charred body. All the things that had caused her so much bother, so much concern, all those things were now gone.

The clown had stayed up all night and through the morning, watching people go in and out of the house over the road. Around midday, he went and stood outside. The rain had cleared up and the sun was now shining blankly, coldly, on the street. After a time the DJ came out to join him. The clown said, How do you think it happened? I don't know, the DJ replied, both of them gazing into the black house, through the empty window frames, I heard one of the people last night saying it started in the kitchen. The clown nodded, Did you know her? he asked the DJ, turning to him with a sincere look in his eyes. The DJ met his gaze, Yes, I spoke to her once or twice, she seemed OK. I knew her, the clown said, I knew Carol well. I used to go to Carol's all the time. I used to talk to her. I knew all her hopes, I knew all her dreams. I was with Carol when the fire started. I told her to run, I told her to get going, but she wouldn't. The DJ looked incredulous. You mean you could have saved her? he said to the clown, emotion rising in his voice. You don't understand, the clown replied, Carol is the name of my dog!

The bear has always found supermarkets difficult to deal with. His concept of objects is in tension with what he finds in a supermarket. In this particular supermarket that he is in he finds a variety of objects. What are they? There is nothing hidden behind them except more of the same. What he sees are not blocks of joined-up characteristics, not just some earth-blob which he is a part of and all the stuff in the supermarket is a part of, distinguishable only through the blind selfishness of his ego. No. There is no such world-blob. In this bear's opinion there is no such world-blob. He sees things that he can group in any infinite number of ways. It is in accordance with these arbitrary groupings that he traverses the aisles of the supermarket. This bear, this particular one, loves to eat some fish, but he rarely begins with fish. He might take a look down the fish aisle and then veer off into an aisle containing cakes or hammers or oil or photographs. The bear carries a basket with him principally to pick up things he needs for his shopping. What he also does is take certain things down from certain shelves and then put them back elsewhere in the supermarket in combinations that make more sense to him. Hence, he places a bottle of sparkling mineral water next to a piece of beef in the meat refrigerator. Next to that, he puts some non-biological washing powder and, balancing on both the washing powder box and the mineral water bottle, forming a kind of bridge over the beef, he puts a multipack pack of crisps. This assemblage is pleasing to him, but still, it lacks something. He spends some time examining it and then walks away. He walks for some time past eggs until he gets to the clothes section of the supermarket. He puts a long white nightgown in his basket and also a bra. He takes a different route back this time, going past some bestselling books and records. He notices a book by popular author Ian McEwan. He picks it up and reads a few words in it, glancing all the time around to see if there are any supermarket staff nearby. Luckily, in their lime-green and orange oversized fleeces they are easy to spot. There are none around, this is what he is able to ascertain. From his basket he pulls out a piece of beef. He puts the beef inside the book and shuts it and returns it to the back of the shelf full of Ian McEwan books. He also puts the bra on an Irvine Welsh book. It doesn't matter which one. Next, going via an aisle containing beer and frozen pizzas, the bear returns to the beef assemblage, which is fortunately still in place. Over the beef, the washing powder box, the sparkling water bottle and the multipack pack of crisps the bear drapes the white nightgown. The assemblage now looks like some abjection of a woman, fallen flat amongst the meat.

He goes nosing around the condiments section and then around packets of dried pasta. There are also pasta sauces. The bear looks up, directly up above him, and sees the cold metal building shell holding them all in, long fat silver tubes and banks of wires. The supermarket sells powders and starches, juices and grapefruits in string bags. Kennels for dogs but not dogs themselves. The bear goes again to the eggs but they make him unhappy. The eggs remind him of a time he cracked open an egg to make a fried egg and in the yolk there seemed to be specks of blood.

The supermarket provides the bear with a superb location for walking around and thinking. It contains visual stimulus enough that the bear does not get bored. The supermarket can be traversed in any number of different ways, offering up combinations of objects and products to think about. The bear walks around and thinks about rosemary, thyme and tea tree handwash. About fennel and pistachio pesto. About blood orange juice.

A constant music comes out of speakers hidden throughout the supermarket. It was the bear's intention at one time to discover the location of these speakers and somehow sabotage them so that they played a different, more resonant music, better suited to his ruminations. Though he followed the music around the store, its vastness, the number of surfaces the sound could bounce off, made discovery of the source impossible.

The bear puts a load of cheese into his basket. Once more he walks down the beef aisle and is disappointed to see a guy in a lime-green fleece with an orange baseball cap dismantling the assemblage, a puzzled look on his face, a tension at the mouth. The bear feels disappointment. He pretends to look at some beef while watching the man. It is a disgrace, he feels, not only that his meaningful collage should have so short a life, but also that this man should be forced to come and work in this airy cage, so cold that he has to put on the ridiculous fleece, the orange hat, forced to tidy up. The bear goes away. In an aisle containing men's jackets the bear fills the men's jacket pockets with cheese.

The Recruitment Consultant, hands tucked neatly behind her back, thumb worrying at the gold band on her finger, which shines, shoes squeaking on the teal floor underneath them, hair plumped and shiny, glances with something like concern at the nurse, the Sister. She is being told about Jack. He's really very fragile, he needs a lot of rest at the moment. The doctor will be round to check on him at one, and he naps after that, so you can only have till then, she trills, all efficiency. The Recruitment Consultant looks at the nurse, sensing a silence needing to be filled. Till one, right, of course, she goes, and . . . forgive me for asking but how will I be able to communicate with him. I mean, will I . . . she trails off. The nurse smiles kindly. O, she replies, well. The stroke was really quite severe. You see, he's no longer able to talk properly. The Recruitment Consultant just smiles back, knowing this all already but savouring the nurse's discomfort, savouring the anticipation, traversing this long hallway. They pass through what must be the twentieth set of double doors and the nurse stops. Well, she says, this is him. If you'd find it more comfortable I can have someone sit in with you. The Recruitment Consultant appears to consider this. No, she replies, no. Jack and I have always got on well. I'll be fine, thank you. She goes in.

The room is painted in thick, textured daubs. It is magnolia. There is a chair. On the TV, which is very loud, a cowboy runs around in a landscape entirely brown in composition. There is a table, there is a vase. These are in the corner. On the table, beside the vase, there is a radio. There is a window covered in droplets and the residue left by droplets. There is a bed with teal sheets and high bars on the sides. There is a wheelchair in the centre that is facing the television. Inside it is Jack. There is a damp smell. The Recruitment Consultant walks to the window and looks out. She walks to the bed and tests its springiness with the palm of her right hand. It is a very springy bed. She goes over to the television and turns the volume right down to silent. She does not look at him yet. She walks to the table. From her purse she takes a cassette which she puts into the radio and switches on. It is Frank Sinatra singing 'September Song'. She turns it up. She takes the chair and turns it round so that it is facing the wheelchair. She goes behind the wheelchair and turns it so that it is facing the chair directly. For a moment she waits there, looking at the empty teal plastic chair. Then she goes and sits in it.

Well now, Jack. She looks at him as she speaks. She gets up again and takes her bag from the floor and places it on the bed. She goes to the TV and switches it off. She sits again. She turns her grin to Jack as if offering a benediction. She opens her hands, speaks again. Here we are. Again she gets up and goes to the window, not really looking out of it. She takes off her coat and lays it on the bed, next to the bag. She adjusts the chair slightly, but does not sit on it, instead wandering around the room while she speaks. Now, Jack, we can't have you watching all those repeats, can we? She pauses. All that crap. But . . . she stops, looking at him. You do look well, you know, Jack. You look much better than I expected. She relishes saying the name, having never really called him anything before. It feels sickly in her mouth; she pronounces it sycophantically, she pronounces it with relish. Her hands are on her hips, her legs slightly apart. You know, she continues, I almost envy you. I do. All this free time on your hands now. You know, I never envied you before today, and I thought, coming in here, that I might pity you. But, ah, no, not really. You seem to have it pretty good here, Jack. But you shouldn't waste your time with the TV; I don't know who has authorised that. I'm sure it's not what you want. When the nurse told me you spent most of your day watching that rubbish I was disappointed, saddened to hear it, Jack, I have to say. Of course, they haven't the staff to read to you. I had thought about bringing you some books, but I anticipated this. A shame, a real shame, I wish, in a way, that I had more time to spend here, there's a great deal that you should have read by now, Jack. A great deal. And now you have the time but not the capacity. Time has turned against you, it's the great irony of disease, you used to never have enough, I never have enough, but now, now you have too much. You have all this time but nothing to do with it. Boredom. The doctors tell me boredom is a great killer, Jack, and all that TV, it must be boring you to death, if you'll excuse the pun. She turns and puts her hands behind her back, looking at the glass in the window. The sun has come out. Below them is the courtyard. Opposite three more walls of wards.

◆

She looks at him now, turns and stares. The skin grey, bristles crisp against the chin, colourless hair splayed out, slept on awkwardly, striped cotton pyjamas, open enough at the neck to show a glimpse of stiff chest hair. Jack stares back at her, jaw slackened, the lips moist, the teeth bitter yellow, and she stares at him. There is no sign of recognition. She stands for a moment as Sinatra sings the refrain. Do you know this song, Jack? I doubt you do. Perhaps you do. Do you know that it's your son's favourite song? He doesn't know I've done this. In fact, I'll let you in on a little secret, he doesn't know I'm here. He thinks I'm on a team-building exercise. But! This song. Do you know he has spent years collecting versions of this song. He has so many. When we were first together we used to trawl around car boot sales and record fairs all the time. Any time we visited a new town we would visit the record shops. He was obsessed with the song for a long time. She is at the window now. She checks her watch. In the centre of the courtyard is a planted area in the shape of a rectangle, rhododendrons, winter-dormant now, with crisp-brown petals and stalks in the grey soil. Around the plants the remainder of the courtyard is concreted over. Two benches stand facing each other from opposite sides and a faint drizzle falls on them and the concrete and on two nurses huddled in their coats, smoking cigarettes and sharing a packet of smoky bacon crisps. She goes and sits on the bed. She picks up her bag and looks inside it. She looks up at the side of Jack's head. She speaks. I think it's a shame you've had so few visitors, a real shame. The nurse told me that only your sister and her children have been so far, myself excepted, of course. A great shame. But you see, as I was mulling over your current situation I came to the realisation that you are something like a blank space, Jack. Your personality has been eroded, all that exist now are fragments, and without you to tie them together, they no longer contain the same resonances. Do you follow me, Jack? What I'm saying is that the truth about you has become subjective, open to inter-pretation. Suddenly now, with you in this state, if I say you are something, then you become it, since you are unable to disagree – or agree – with me. So if I tell the nurses that, Oh, I don't know, you were a great fan of the work of Monet, then what reason would they have for disagreeing with me? And if I brought in a Monet print and asked if it would be OK to hang it above your bed – well then, you see, it seems to become the truth that you are a lover of Monet. For why would I lie about something like that? But that's a very sim-plistic example, Jack, of how you are a blank space. Let me outline it for you in a slightly more complicated way. Let's say I was to visit your house now – Oh, by the way, Richard has given me his key, so I may pay a visit to the place. I understand you're keeping it till you die, a good decision, I think, but that's by the by. If I visited your house and sifted through your belongings, there would be evidence of a life, things you have owned, treasured, the detritus of existence. Perhaps you see already what I'm getting at, Jack. Let's say I've never known you, but somehow I gain access to your house now. There is plenty of evidence to suggest the kind of life you lead, the kind of man that you are, but on its own the evidence is difficult to decode. How am I, never having met you, to know which things you thought most important, which most beautiful, which had sentimental value and for what reasons? I could make a judgement, but it would be based as much upon my prejudices, my own likes and dislikes as anything else. And if somebody else came along the next day and went through your house similarly, they might conceive of you as an entirely different person. Do you see what I mean? Now let's imagine an alternative scenario where I, like before, am somebody who has never met you, and for whatever reason, you, by which I mean you before you became ill, decide to give me a tour of your house to show me the sort of man you are. Now, there are things you would show me, things you would be able to tell stories about, some things you would spend a lot of time on, others very little time, indeed there may be things that you would conceal from me, not wanting them to influence the way that I thought about you. After you had finished, well, it would still be up to me to make my judgement, and yes, it would still be based upon my own prejudices, my own idiosyncrasies as before, but the fact of your autonomy over the situation changes everything, the fact that I encountered you among your possessions is crucial to my impression, because what I will be judging is less the things themselves and more your reaction to them and your reaction to me. What I would focus on would be the way you told me things, what you chose to elaborate on and what you were reluctant to discuss. I hope my meaning is becoming clearer to you now, Jack, because you see, now that you are in this state, the possibility of that autonomy, that control over how people judge you, has disappeared. And, perhaps I am out on a limb a little here, Jack, but see what you think; it is that autonomy that makes us human. You're a little like a book by an unknown author. You are a non-person now, Jack, you're not a man any more.

She grins. Jack remains in place. He is inscrutable. His eyeballs barely move. She gets up from the bed and sits back down on the chair facing him. She grins. This situation puts me in a unique position, Jack. Unlike all the staff here, I knew you before you were ill, so whatever I say to people here about you, they're likely to believe me. To them you are just a cipher, just a body. The Recruitment Consultant pauses again, gazing at Jack, whose face remains inert, his body limp like papier-mâché stuffed with mincemeat. I think that they enjoy hearing stories about you, anecdotes, anything, it makes you seem more human – otherwise you might as well have been born like this. Though one might say that anyway, this is all your life has amounted to, this is all you'll ever become, Jack. You are a blank canvas and whatever I throw at you will stick.

She gets up. She goes behind the wheelchair and turns it so it faces the bed. She goes and sits on the bed. She lolls back, one crooked arm supporting her. She faces the artex ceiling. Your son loves this song. The singer has changed, it is now Robert Wyatt, but he is still singing 'September Song'. Ah, yes. She blinks contentedly. Jack, this is Robert Wyatt, a man who spent much of his life in a wheelchair. Well, this is actually a fairly recent version of the song.

I think you can tell that if you listen closely. Wyatt plays it very straight, he looks for the genuine pathos, the true humanity of the song. You see, what dates many of the older versions is the schmaltziness of them. You don't get the feeling that the singers really mean or even fully understand what they're singing. They're just doing the song because it's the sort of song that singers like them are expected to do and they embellish it with vocal tricks and oversinging. But not Wyatt, he sings it as plaintive as possible. The arrangement serves a similar purpose – it's by a man called Pascal Comelade – very downbeat, very evocative. He even cuts out the first section of the song, which you'll hear in some of the other versions on the tape. He has a wonderful voice, don't you think? The words sound genuine, fatigued, you really think that the days he sings about are becoming more and more precious and that the 'you' he is addressing is Wyatt's own true-life partner. Do you know the song? It's 'September Song'. I went to the trouble of selecting my favourites from Richard's collection and putting them on this tape for you.

She gets up from the bed and goes to the window. Have you looked at the view much, Jack? Shall we have a look at this view? She goes again to the wheelchair and pushes it along so that the man's face is looking out the window. It is hard to know if he is hearing or understanding anything. Well then, Jack, there you are. This is it; this is what it amounts to, in the final analysis. This is all you'll see of the outside world until you die, this concrete box. Behind her, the Recruitment Consultant hears the click of the door and the swish of it being quietly opened. Without looking round, without appearing to notice, she continues. It's all too brief a time we have, Jack, but you've lived well and this is not an ignominious end, not by any means, it is in fact a rather noble finish, a … The Recruitment Consultant hears a polite feminine cough behind her and turns around swiftly on the ball of one foot. In front of the door she sees a young nurse, thin, almost frail looking, white skin, curly black hair, slender arms, tiny wrists. Yes?

I'm sorry, miss, I was just asked to check in to make sure everything's OK with you two and to remind you that the doctor is coming round at one. She sounds nervous. The Recruitment Consultant takes a couple of steps towards her. Well, thank you, er – she steps forward again and leans down towards the nurse's breast to read her name tag – Claire. Thank you, Claire. We are fine; Jack and I were just admiring the view. I'm sure it's a wonderful garden in the summer.

Yes, the residents enjoy it, replies the nurse, Perhaps if you visit again when the weather's better you could take Jack out there. She gazes up at the Recruitment Consultant's beaming face, a little apprehensive. Yes, yes, I'm sure he'd like that. The Recruitment Consultant glances back at the wheelchair, which is still facing in the opposite direction, Jack's blank eyes gazing out at the opposite wall, which contains a number of windows that show rooms identical to his. The Recruitment Consultant leans in towards the nurse, speaking in a whisper, but not so quiet that Jack cannot hear. I fear he may not make it long enough to see the flowers here bloom. Claire looks at her quizzically, a little confused by this remark, but the Recruitment Consultant keeps smiling at her, eyes locked on hers while the nurse tries to avoid meeting them, scrutinising various bits of carpet and wall. Well, I appreciate your concern, Claire, I thank you for it. Was there anything else? Yes, actually, Claire replies. The Sister just wanted to ask whether Jack's son will be visiting at all? It's in the register that he scheduled a visit but then cancelled, is that right? The Recruitment Consultant sours her grin, but inwardly thanks her for the question.

Yes, that is correct, Claire, he did schedule an appointment a few weeks ago, but he won't be visiting Jack, not ever, I'm afraid. I've tried to talk to him about it but he's adamant, there's no way. The Recruitment Consultant pauses, returning the grin to her face. Claire doesn't seem to know how to react, just about managing a choked-out Oh, but the Recruitment Consultant continues, electric with the sense of the moment. Yes. You see, Claire. She moves her face even further towards the nurse, who seems repulsed, but either too afraid or too intrigued to move she stays stock still, her feet planted together. Jack, she pauses again, as if unsure how exactly to word what she has to say. She tilts her face suddenly up to the ceiling and keeps it there as she says: Jack . . . did something to Richard, when he was younger. Long before I ever met him, something terrible. He won't ever tell me what, not until Jack is dead. He's scared of what I might do to him if I ever found out. The Recruitment Consultant returns her face to Claire's, which is whiter than ever. Her grin has disappeared and her voice drops and becomes grave. So you see, Claire,

I'm visiting in Richard's place. Jack and I always got on. I consider it an act of goodwill. But I'm afraid you'll have to tell the Sister that Jack's son won't be visiting. Is that what you wanted to know? Claire snaps back to attention at the question, flustered, Yes. Thank you, I'll tell her. Thanks. O, Claire, there was something I wanted as well, the Recruitment Consultant adds. Yes? Claire looks uncertainly at the Recruitment Consultant. Well, it's like this, you see. I come in here today and I see Jack watching the television. The problem is that Jack always hated TV. I think after his wife died he got rid of their set. He could never stand television. O? Yes. So I think having to sit here watching it must be torture for him. Claire, are you familiar with this music? The Recruitment Consultant gestures towards the radio, which is now playing a Hawaiian version of the song. Claire looks blank. It's 'September Song', a classic, a standard. Claire, Jack was always a great fan of music, and this was his favourite song, he was forever playing this tape when I went round, he said he found it very comforting. So I went to the trouble of going round there earlier and picking up the tape to bring here for him. I think it would be in Jack's best interests if you removed the TV from the room and just played the tape for him. All it would take is for somebody to come in every three-quarters of an hour to turn it over. Would that be OK? I know the song means a great deal to Jack, she grinned. I don't think that would be a problem, I'll go tell Sister, says the nurse. Thank you. Goodbye Claire. It was pleasant to have met you. The Recruitment Consultant beams at Claire who manages the trace of a smile as she leaves.

Well then, Jack. Now there's a girl for you. A lovely figure. I wonder if you still feel desire. Is that something you still feel, Jack? Of course there can be no physical manifestation, but the mind does not often recognise our bodily limitations when it comes to matters like that now, does it? The Recruitment Consultant, back next to Jack, turns and grins at him, winking like a leery uncle. I don't suppose it matters. If you feel any desire for her it can only be one frustration among thousands, just one more thing that you'll never be able to do again. Of course, even before your illness she would never want somebody like you. You always dressed too cheaply, Jack, you didn't talk well enough. A girl like that, you have to take some interest. And to her now, what are you? Just a body, just a lump of ugly, diseased flesh. You are just a job to her. She resents you, I'm sure of it. I can usually tell these things. She turns away from Jack and back to the window; the sun is shining on the brown rhododendrons below. Now where were we, Jack? We were talking about the view, yes. Look out there. Do you see those windows? Behind each of them is another person like you; another incapacitated man or woman waiting to die. If you wait here till night-time and they switch their lights on and you have your lights on in here – I notice there are no curtains in these rooms – if you wait here then, perhaps, someone else on the other side of the courtyard will be waiting there in front of the window, sitting in their chair just like you. And your eyes might meet. Of course, the possibility of all this happening is, as with everything that's going to happen to you for the rest of your life, completely out of your control, but if it were to happen, Jack, then I think that would be the most potent form of human communication you are ever likely to experience again. Yes.

You know, Jack, what I said to the nurse there was correct. Richard won't be visiting you, not ever. The reason he hasn't visited you since Elaine died is that he can't stand you. You remember the nice reading he gave at Elaine's funeral? There will be none of that for you. We won't be going to your funeral, neither of us. Actually, you know what, I did tell a tiny lie to the nurse a moment ago, Richard has told me everything you did to him, hasn't omitted a thing. And you know, Jack, he has had to physically wrench me from the phone, or hide my car keys to stop me getting to you, that much is true. God knows, Jack, I am a small woman, a weak person. On 'weak' the Recruitment Consultant seems to force down a lump in her throat but she keeps going, eyes fixed on the rhododendrons below. I have held back in front of you, made small talk, pretended things were all right, pretended I relished your company even, and I think you believed me. But, Jack, listen to me now, if you'd have seen him on those nights, if you had had any idea. But of course you have no idea what you did to him, you haven't the slightest clue – if you were capable of knowing then you would never have done those things in the first place. It's fitting you've ended up this way, Jack, I think it's very apt. She forces a grin. I think it's a fair reflection. But, Jack, I may be a small person, but not so small as to make all this about me, I'm not here for some ridiculous conflict, I'm not here for revenge. You realise the position of power that I'm in here, Jack, don't you? I could do anything. But I'm not like that. I am not so small, Jack, to have not questioned the ethics of this situation. I'm talking to a disabled man, someone who can't reply, can't refute what I say, can't interrupt either physically or verbally. You can see how this situation would reflect badly on me if somebody unaware of the context were to be watching. Believe me, Jack, this behaviour is not spontaneous, it took a great deal of contemplation. I struggled with my conscience. You can believe that, can't you? I feel that now I'm only doing what is completely necessary. It's something you've had coming to you for some time. I've been wanting to say this for a long time, Jack, but the problem is you were never a very good listener, were you, Jack? But, that's all changed now, that's one good thing that's come out of all this, don't you think? I like to think so. As I say, I think it's fitting that you're going to die like this. She turns the chair away from the window and crouches down so that she is level with Jack's ruined face. Their eyes are locked on each other. Well, Jack. Here we are. And would you believe, I told that nurse another little fib? It's just a small thing, Jack, but I think I'd better tell you. When I said you probably wouldn't last to see the rhododendrons down there bloom, I wasn't being entirely truthful – I said that for Claire's benefit. Jack, believe me, I'm not here to make you think that you don't have long left, quite the contrary in fact. I got talking to your doctor on the way in, a very nice guy, very genial. You see, Jack, you will see the flowers outside bloom, and you'll see winter again in this place. The doctor predicts that you'll live for several more years like this. A decade even. But Jack, if you think you're in pain now then you're mistaken. He said that your condition can only grow worse, your future is nothing but pain, intense pain. Soon, quite soon really, just a couple of years away, the pain will be so great that, if you could speak, you'd be begging for someone to slip you an overdose, you'll want so desperately to be able to end it, Jack, but no one will help you. Midway through her sentence the tape clicks off for the end of the first side. The Recruitment Consultant rises and moves over to the machine, slowly and deliberately she turns the tape over and presses play again. The tune starts up, this time a singer with a French accent tackles the opening lines, and the Recruitment Consultant goes and crouches down in front of the chair, her face set hard, looking disgusted at what's in front of her. Nobody cares enough to take that risk for you, Jack. She rises again and puts her hands in her pockets. She smiles. Well then, Jack, I think that's about all, I think I've said everything I came here to say. I can't say you've been very good company, but then I don't think I could ever say that about you. She picks up her bag and gathers up her coat from the bed. I hope you enjoy your tape, Jack, you're going to be hearing a lot of it from now on. She goes to the door and opens it a little way. Now, Jack, perhaps I'll come again, in a few years' time, in the summer, and take you for a turn around the garden. We'll see. Whatever happens, I know I'll be thinking of you. Perhaps you might take a few moments each day to think of me as well, I'd appreciate that. Well, goodbye then, Jack. The Recruitment Consultant looks once more at the old man in the chair. She shuts the door.

Out in the hallway, the Recruitment Consultant encounters the nurse and a man introduced as Doctor Benson, who is responsible for Jack's treatment. The Recruitment Consultant grins deferentially. Benson looks at her with sympathy. How did you find today? he asks, I know a lot of people find the first few times difficult. O, well, Jack and I have always got on very well, as I think I said to the Sister, we have a rapport, you know. Talking to him today I found myself almost able to fill in what Jack would have said, it wasn't so different. Well, that's good, that's very good, said the doctor. Tell me, doctor – if I can ask candidly – how long does he have left? Well, it's very hard to say, um, he's in a very fragile state at the moment, so he's particularly susceptible to illnesses. His immune system has been significantly weakened, so any disease would be a big threat to him. That said, he could just as easily last another year, or longer. Cases like Jack's are very difficult to predict. The Recruitment Consultant nods gravely and looks at the tiled floor for some seconds. Well, thank you for your time and all you're doing for Jack here. I'll let you get on. Goodbye, doctor. Sister. The Recruitment Consultant smiles at them both.

The door clinks open in front of the Recruitment Consultant. She lets an old lady, hair and coat soaking wet, go past her and then steps out into the murk, heels clicking on the wet tarmac. Shielding the match from the wind she lights up a cigarette and takes a couple of drags looking up at the sky and at the people bustling round the carpark like pinballs, slaves to the wind. She smokes only half of it before flicking it away, watching the slender arc it describes in the air. A faint wisp of sun seems to be struggling through the cloud, and if the sun, though only the winter sun, is going to shine today, then who else could it shine on but the Recruitment Consultant, who walks right past her car, leaves the car park and goes out in the direction of those few little shafts of sunlight that hover uncertainly over the damp pavement.

It is a spring evening and the bear decides to attend a public lecture at the university. It is entitled *The Postmodern Palimpsest: Breviary, Boundary and Taxonomy in the New Fiction*. The lecture is to be followed by a presentation from some practitioners of this new fiction. The bear does not go along alone. He brings a friend who is working on a PhD, the subject of which is Aphorisms in George Eliot's *Middlemarch*. This guy, his name is Steven, is telling the bear all about Casaubon's proposed *Key to All Mythologies*, when a hush descends as a fat and red old man takes the stage. He spends some moments in the silence fiddling with some buttons behind the lectern until the right-hand screen of the two in the auditorium lights up and displays the title of the lecture in a large black sans-serif font. The professor then walks to the front row and speaks to a man with a laptop in front of him. The left-hand screen lights up and a blinking cursor appears. The professor looks at it and the man types and the word 'hello' appears on the screen in the same sans-serif font. It is then highlighted and deleted. The professor walks back to the lectern, his hands in the pockets of his grey-green trousers. Reaching the lectern, he picks up a remote control device in his right hand and presses a button on it. On the right-hand screen appears a quotation from John Cage. It is the score for his 'Variations III': For one or any number of people performing any actions. The professor walks away from the lectern and turns and looks at the screen, his back to the audience, his hand on his chin. After a time he turns back to the audience and opens his arms and eyes wide and declaims: Conceive of a book, the pages of which are made of acetate and the symbols on each page themselves are meaningless, but particular combinations of those pages would reveal different legible texts. Yes? As the professor speaks, the man with the laptop types at pace and on the left-hand screen, the professor's words appear moments after he says them. The typing is not perfect, and there are many spelling errors, grammatical errors, syntactical errors and typographical errors throughout. Nevertheless, the bear finds himself watching the accumulation of characters on the screen as much as listening to what's being said. The professor: Consider now a book in which the plane of incidence is three-dimensionally perpendicular to the page so (here the professor clicks his remote control and the screen displays a pink slashed egg-shaped canvas by Lucio Fontana) the writing goes down into the book. Conceive of that. How might we read such a book? And what implications might such a reading have? The codex form is rooted in early Christian theism, which forces one to wonder what a truly atheistic text might look like. Conceive of a two-dimensional book with one constantly shifting glyph. Conceive of a spherical book, yes?, which can be begun at any point and read in any direction. Such books, I have no doubt, will being to appear on our shelves in the next ten years. Steven, grinning, turns to the bear and rolls his eyes and whispers, And will roll off our shelves too! In spite of himself, the bear grins. The man in the row in front of the bear and Steven turns round and glares at Steven and the bear from behind his glasses. In his right hand he clutches a narrowly coiled coil of paper tightly wound around a central spool. The bear can make out the words 'Metaphor is never, in fact, an . . .' written on the paper, before the writing is obscured by the man's fingers.

The professor's colour is high. He clicks his little remote control and brings up a quotation from John Leland: (. . .) to fragment presupposes some whole in the first place capable of being fragmented, just as the fragment, incomplete in itself, presupposes a whole or 'totality' which completes it. Again the professor looks at the screen and seems to ruminate on it. The clicking of the keyboard is temporarily silent. Until the professor barks: Yes. Yes. Consider a book so placed as to reveal itself as you walk around the modern urban city, a book intrinsically bound up in the environmental circumstances of its production. How might such a book be read and spoken of? What happens to such a book if your bus is late? Consider a book which has thick fat pages that you can scratch away to reveal new elements and near-infinite combinations of text. What would be the significance of the construction of such a book, of such an enmeshment of quotation? The current failure in fiction is a failure of imagination. It is a failure that we do not yet have books literally as physically large and imposing as skyscrapers. The failure is that we do not yet have a book that can both literally AND figuratively pick up a saxophone and jam along with Hendrix or Cobain or whoever else. A book that can literally go into a bar and pick up a woman and make love to that woman. We need such a book, yes? Hands everywhere. A book that could talk to them, tell them the things they want to know. A book that could put the right music on, or talk about the right music. Sometimes I think that I want that so much. This book. I don't . . . The professor pauses and scratches his head. He looks up at the left-hand screen which displays what he has just said. There is a gulf between it, that text and him, that man. Looking at it he seems confused. He clicks his remote control once more. The right-hand screen now says this: 'Metaphor is never, in fact, an innocent figure of speech. – Alain Robbe-Grillet.' The professor looks at it, looks back at the left-hand screen which still displays what he just said and a blinking, expectant cursor, ready to record whatever he says again. He looks back to the right-hand screen and again to the left. Ah yes, he booms. Ah. Now . . . there is a pause. He starts to speak again so rapidly that the typist struggles to keep up, starts to miss out words, starts to make more mistakes. I want to talk about the novel today. The novel as it is. The book as it is. Imagine that I am today's book. I am some corporeal transformation into the book today, some embodiment of it. The professor walks right to the front of the stage and raises both his hands so that they are level with his face. His four fingers together and the thumb below, the construction is a little like a mouth, and the professor turns to each mouth, smiling. Now, he says, speaking more gently now, now, in order to talk about current narrative, I am going to use Righty and Lefty here. Is that OK with you, Righty? Righty, which is the professor's right hand, has a high-pitched American accent, a little like how Mickey Mouse talks, Well gee, sure, says Righty, that'd be swell. The professor asks Lefty how he feels about the situation. Lefty has a low, American accent, from somewhere in the south. He sounds a bit like how you imagine Lenny in *Of Mice and Men* to sound. Lefty says, Uhh, uh huh, yup yup, OK. The professor says, Thank you, Lefty. Hey, what about me? Righty interjects. And thank you too, Righty, says the professor. Righty mumbles something inaudible. The typist, evidently close enough to hear it, transcribes it as 'You prick'.

Righty begins to speak again, only this time in a soft Yorkshire burr: It was late, it was dark, I came stumbling through the park. I had too much to drink, I was not dry. I saw dogs out the corner of my eye. I saw them coming from my bleary mark. All the dogs began to bark.

Now Lefty speaks. He has the voice of Alan Sugar: On the sofa were three. In her headphones was jazz. In her headphones was rap. The curtains were drawn to stop the glare of the sun on the TV screen, which was showing adverts. In her headphones was a pop song, an old one. They were sat on the sofa reading books. The TV was also on, showing adverts. Opposite the window, on a dressing table, was a mirror with three panels that reflected nine faces, nine haircuts, nine shoulders, nine books. In the first book a man said, as she read, 'Yes, that all seems in order.' While the third read, 'In the narrow gully between the backs of houses, permanently damp from the overflowing drains of the houses, the water greasy with yellowing washing-up suds. He picked his way among the snaking streams of water brown with the juice of fried meat, or white with the scum of scrubbed-off bath skin.' The second read this: 'It's good to finally see you.'

One got up, leaving only six behind. The TV was showing a rap video. In her headphones was rap, still. The sun had gone in, so she opened the curtains. Three children, outside, dropped three ice-creams and three red balloons drifted into the sky.

Righty (generic Scandinavian): You were wearing a baggy suit and a white shirt. You told me you had just lost your job. I told you it wouldn't be so bad. You didn't agree. Call me, OK?

Lefty (high-pitched, childish): Malcolm glanced at the Glock, which was hard and black. He knew Graham would shoot. He knew that about Graham because he knew that Graham was that kind of man. Graham was a hard man. Malcolm knew that. It's your move, Malcolm, Graham said. His voice sounded like gravel when he spoke. This was because he was a hard man. I know, replied Malcolm. Malcolm knew. Malcolm knew Graham was a bad man. A hard man. He knew that. It's too late, Malcolm, said Graham. As Graham said that he cocked the gun. Malcolm knew it was too late for him. It was too late for Malcolm because of Graham. BANG BANG BANG.

Righty (posh old woman): I met Michael Jackson only once. I was in a shop. I was looking at the magazines, in particular a magazine I wanted which was about cookery. Michael Jackson came in. I think he was with his bodyguards. He is remarkably dark-skinned in the flesh. Remarkably so. Still, I knew full well it was him. I felt that profoundly. Michael Jackson came up to me and asked me all about my dental history. Why, Michael, I said to him, I have had some work done, but my teeth are good. Then I let Michael Jackson look at my teeth. He paid them a lot of attention. He was particularly fond of my incisors. I agreed with him that I have particularly good incisors. With the flat white pads of his fingers he felt all around my molars. It felt good, to have him feel there. It felt so good.

Lefty begins to relate a story about a gigantic egg in the voice of Margaret Thatcher when Righty, in an almost indecipherably thick French accent, interjects and the two talk over each other, getting louder and louder, their voices changing and becoming indistinguishable. It's difficult to tell who is saying what or which side of the argument you should be on. The professor's eyes dart from Lefty to Righty and back again. The two seem to break free of his control and come together, snapping and biting at each other until the professor, struggling, yanks them apart and, finally opens his hands. There is absolute silence in the room. The professor stands there looking down at his palms, disbelief in his eyes and his mouth just a scant red O. This goes on for some minutes and the audience begins to murmur. The typist scrolls back through the barrage of text he has just transcribed, fixing typos and spelling errors as best he can while there is silence. Eventually the professor turns and looks at the screen. He clicks his little remote once more. A triptych comes onto the screen. The left panel of the triptych is a painting in the style of Francis Bacon. It shows a room with a red floor and a grey wall. A black rectangle in the upper right corner suggests a window at night. There is a round brown table not in proper perspective upon which there is a red lamp that gives off a red glow. In the middle of the painting is the vestige of a man in a black suit, except that his face is smeared away. OK says the professor. OK. The central panel of the triptych is a black and white photograph of a woman with a dog on a lead looking to her left. To her right appears to be a bright apparition, a daub of spectral light that the dog is looking intently at. Let's talk now about blankness, he says. Let's talk now about what I like to call stylistic blankness. He stressed the word 'stylistic' by making his voice go almost into falsetto when saying it. The typist goes back and highlights it and puts the word in italics to reflect this stressing. The right-hand panel of the triptych is a crowd photograph in colour, taken at a club or at a gig. It shows a mass of happy-looking faces and some hands raised up in celebration.

The professor clicks his remote control and a picture of a document appears on the screen. The writing is very small and, to the bear at least, from his distance, illegible. The professor turns and looks at the text on the screen for some time. He turns back to the audience. My teeth hurt, he says. It is unclear if he is quoting anybody.

◆

The land I occupied is going downhill he said.

Sometimes my partner and I argue he said.

Truth first joy first grace third, charity, hope, faith, judgement, suffering all third, love, peace first, goal slash end, mercy, shame, shame he said.

Body foot hand face mouth eye blood flesh member limb he said.

Notice a lot of abstract nouns are feminine he said.

Household father mother daughter son second husband wife slash woman leader king he said.

Fire water light night star age name will year mountains slash hill he said.

We all went out he said.

Her tits were like . . . I paused he said.

It was the night time he said.

The clothes I wore came from town he said.

Dad he said.

He said they said I slash they see having come we ate you singular fell you suffered you plural threw I slash they took slash received I slash they had I went down I slash they left he knew I slash they drank he fled you plural found it happened slash he became I slash they lead I slash they died I slash they learned I slash they sinned I slash they carried he said.

The professor does a little jump. He presses his remote and just a blank screen comes up. He looks at what the typist has just typed, which is what he has just said. He smiles at the audience. Well, he says wearily, that concludes this particular part of the presentation. I urge you to stay on and listen to some practitioners of the new fiction present their exciting new work which to my mind renegotiates some of the territory we've been dealing with in new and innovative ways that expand the borders of what the book might be in our times. The professor leaves the stage.

A man walks onto the stage carrying a video camera. He sets the camera up on a tripod so that it is facing the stage. He goes over to the lectern and opens a door at the front with his key. He pulls out a wire and attaches it to the video camera. He goes to the computer behind the lectern and presses some buttons. On the right-hand screen the image of the empty stage appears. The man goes in front of the camera and waves his hand in front of the lens while looking at the right-hand screen. On the right-hand screen a giant hand waves up and down.

The man leaves.

Several middle-aged women walk onto the stage. They all wear brown swimming costumes, brown swimming caps and goggles. One of them, the central woman, steps forward. She looks to the left of the auditorium and enunciates clearly. Please visit our website, she says. She looks to the centre of the auditorium. Please visit our website, she says. She looks to the right of the auditorium. Please visit our website, she says. She steps back. The left-hand woman steps forward. We each have one story, she says to the left of the auditorium. We each have one story, she says to the centre of the auditorium. We each have one story, she says to the right of the auditorium. She steps back.

Another woman steps forward. Sorry I kept you all waiting, she says to the left of the auditorium. Sorry I kept you all waiting, she says to the right of the auditorium. Sorry I kept you all waiting, she says to the centre of the auditorium. On the projected screen, the phrase appears three times.

My name is Kate, she says.
My name is Kate.
My name is Kate.

Is my voice clear enough?
Is my voice clear enough?
Is my voice clear enough?

Before you leave today, I would like to say a couple of
things.
Before you leave today, I would like to say a couple of
things.
Before you leave today, I would like to say a couple of
things.

I hope you have a good bank holiday weekend.
I hope you have a good bank holiday weekend.
I hope you have a good bank holiday weekend.

At this point, another woman from the line steps forward
and addresses both the speaker and the audience.

Are you going anywhere? she asks.
Are you going anywhere?
Are you going anywhere?

The speaker looks at her interlocutor and then back at
the audience.

Mary said, Am I going anywhere? she says.
Mary said, Am I going anywhere?
Mary said, Am I going anywhere?

Yes, I'm going to Alton Towers.
Yes, I'm going to Alton Towers.
Yes, I'm going to Alton Towers.

Whatever you may be doing . . . she pauses as one of the

women in brown interrupts. She turns to the interrupter.
Louise?

She must have lots of money, Louise says.
She must have lots of money.
She must have lots of money.

The speaker looks at her interlocutor and then back at
the audience.

Louise says I must have lots of money, she says.
Louise says I must have lots of money.
Louise says I must have lots of money.

No, it's a treat from my son.
No, it's a treat from my son.
No, it's a treat from my son.

Louise interrupts again.

Your son must be well off then, she exclaims.
Your son must be well off then!
Your son must be well off then!

The speaker looks at Louise and then turns back to the
audience.

Louise says my son must be well off, she says.
Louise says my son must be well off.
Louise says my son must be well off.

No, he just lost his job.
No, he just lost his job.
No, he just lost his job.

Whatever you may be doing, take care and keep safe, she says.
Whatever you may be doing, take care and keep safe.
Whatever you may be doing, take care and keep safe.

Mary says, OK Kate.
OK Kate.
OK Kate.

Cut, exclaims Kate.
Cut!
Cut!

Kate returns to her place in the line and Louise steps forward.

Good afternoon, she says.
Good afternoon.
Good afternoon.

Is my voice clear enough?
Is my voice clear enough?
Is my voice clear enough?

I have new wall tiles in my kitchen!
I have new wall tiles in my kitchen!

I have new wall tiles in my kitchen!

At this point, Kate signals that she wants to ask a question by raising her right arm.

Kate?
Kate?
Kate?

What colour are they, Louise? Kate asks.
What colour are they, Louise?
What colour are they?

Kate is asking what colour they are, Louise explains.
Kate is asking what colour they are.
Kate is asking what colour they are.

They are cream.
They are cream.
They are cream.

Another woman, one who hasn't spoken before, wants to ask a question now.

Who put them up, Louise? she asks.
Who put them up, Louise?
Who put them up, Louise?

Penny wants to know who put them up, Louise says.
Penny wants to know who put them up.

Penny wants to know who put them up.

My husband Kevin.
My husband Kevin.
My husband Kevin.

Yet another woman who has not yet spoken interrupts.

Are you decorating your whole house? she asks.
Are you decorating your whole house?
Are you decorating your whole house?

Louise looks at the woman, then looks at the audience.

Carol wants to know if we're decorating the whole house,
she says.
Carol wants to know if we're decorating the whole house.
Carol wants to know if we're decorating the whole house.

No, just the kitchen.
No, just the kitchen.
No, just the kitchen.

They have motifs on them.
They have motifs on them.
They have motifs on them.

One is a butterfly, one is a moth, one is a dragonfly.
One is a butterfly, one is a moth, one is a dragonfly.
One is a butterfly, one is a moth, one is a dragonfly.

My husband knocked a nail into a water pipe.
My husband knocked a nail into a water pipe.
My husband knocked a nail into a water pipe.

That is true, by the way.
That is true, by the way.
That is true, by the way.

Louise returns to her place in the line and another
woman steps forward.

Good afternoon, she says.
Good afternoon.
Good afternoon.

Is my voice at a good level?
Is my voice at a good level?
Is my voice at a good level?

This weekend, I'm going to attack the garden. It's like a
forest.
This weekend, I'm going to attack the garden. It's like a
forest.
This weekend, I'm going to attack the garden. It's like a
forest.

Kate interjects.

Do you have a lot of trees, Barbara? she asks.

Do you have a lot of trees?
Do you have a lot of trees?

The speaker looks at Kate and then back at the audience.

Kate just asked me do I have a lot of trees.
Kate just asked me do I have a lot of trees.
Kate just asked me do I have a lot of trees.

Yes, but they should be bushes!
Yes, but they should be bushes!
Yes, but they should be bushes!

It's also full of litter, the garden.
It's also full of litter, the garden.
It's also full of litter, the garden.

Kate interjects again.

Do you need a new dustbin? she asks.
Do you need a new dustbin?!
Do you need a new dustbin!?

Barbara looks at Kate for a moment and then turns back
towards the audience.

Kate just asked me do I need a new dustbin.
Kate just asked me do I need a new dustbin.
Kate just asked me do I need a new dustbin.

No, I need to educate the people who throw their cans
over my wall.
No, I need to educate the people who throw their cans
over my wall.
No, I need to educate the people who throw their cans
over my wall.

Barbara smiles a bit and returns to her place in the line.

Mary steps forward.

Hello, I'm Mary, she says.
Hello, I'm Mary.
Hello, I'm Mary.

I am meeting Mum tomorrow.
I am meeting Mum tomorrow.
I am meeting Mum tomorrow.

We are having lunch together.
We are having lunch together.
We are having lunch together.

I'm staying with her over the weekend.
I'm staying with her over the weekend.
I'm staying with her over the weekend.

Carol interrupts.

That sounds nice, she says.

That sounds nice.
That sounds nice.

Penny interrupts.

What will you be doing? she asks.
What will you be doing?
What will you be doing?

Mary looks first at Carol and then at Penny and then back
at the audience.

Penny wants to know what we will be doing.
Penny wants to know what we will be doing.
Penny wants to know what we will be doing.

Mum wants a few jobs doing at the bungalow.
Mum wants a few jobs doing at the bungalow.
Mum wants a few jobs doing at the bungalow.

The typist has a great deal of trouble with the spelling of
bungalow, finally having to use his spellchecker to find
the correct organisation of letters. Barbara interrupts.

I hope she's paying you well, she exclaims.
I hope she's paying you well!
I hope she's paying you well!

Mary looks at Barbara and then at the typist. She waits
for the typist to catch up and finish typing the third 'I

hope she's paying you well!' before turning back to the audience.

Barbara said, I hope she's paying you well, she says.
Barbara said, I hope she's paying you well.
Barbara said, I hope she's paying you well.

I do it for nothing, she's my mum.
I do it for nothing, she's my mum.
I do it for nothing, she's my mum.

Louise interrupts.

I hope she's feeding you well, she exclaims.
I hope she's feeding you well!
I hope she's feeding you well!

Mary looks at Louise. She continues to look at Louise.

Yes, she says.
Yes.
Yes.

Mary goes back to the line.

The final woman steps forward. It is Carol. Before Carol speaks, Barbara has something to say.

I was telling Gareth, Carol doesn't need to be recorded.
I was telling Gareth, Carol doesn't need to be recorded.

I was telling Gareth, Carol doesn't need to be recorded.

As she is saying this, the man who set up the camera returns to the stage and presses a button on the camera which causes it to switch off and the right-hand screen to go black.

Now Carol can speak.

Is my voice clear enough? she says.
Is my voice clear enough?
Is my voice clear enough?

Good afternoon.
Good afternoon.
Good afternoon.

At the weekend I will be going out with my family. We're going to Spiral Park.
At the weekend I will be going out with my family. We're going to Spiral Park.
At the weekend I will be going out with my family. We're going to Spiral Park.

Penny interrupts.

Where's that? she asks.
Where's that?
Where's that?

Mary answers.

Penny wants to know where that is.
Penny wants to know where that is.
Penny wants to know where that is.

Carol responds.

It's a local village garden centre.
It's a local village garden centre.
It's a local village garden centre.

At Spiral Park, they have great walks, birds of prey and a
small tea shop.
At Spiral Park, they have great walks, birds of prey and a
small tea shop.
At Spiral Park, they have great walks, birds of prey and a
small tea shop.

Kate has a question now.

Have you been there before, Carol? she asks.
Have you been there before, Carol?
Have you been there before?

Carol turns from Kate back to the audience.

Kate asked whether I'd been there before.
Kate asked whether I'd been there before.
Kate asked whether I'd been there before.

♦

Yes, I have, on a number of occasions.
Yes, I have, on a number of occasions.
Yes, I have, on a number of occasions.

Louise interrupts.

Do they have lots of scrummy things at the teashop?
Do they have lots of scrummy things at the teashop?
Do they have lots of scrummy things at the teashop?

Carol has an answer. She looks at the audience.

Louise wants to know if they have lots of scrummy things
at the teashop.
Louise wants to know if they have lots of scrummy things
at the teashop.
Louise wants to know if they have lots of scrummy things
at the teashop.

Oh yes, they do.
Oh yes, they do.
Oh yes, they do.

Louise has another question.

Would I approve? she asks.
Would I approve?
Would I approve?

✦

Carol looks at Louise. Mary looks at the audience.

Louise wants to know if she would approve.
Louise wants to know if she would approve.
Louise wants to know if she would approve.

Most definitely.
Most definitely.
Most definitely.

Carol rejoins the line. They have all spoken now. The
women all leave the stage. The evening is over.

This job came in. The first guy we got for it was called Timothy. He'd been with us for quite a while; he was one of the guys that was shitlisted. We call it shitlisted. If you're on the shitlist. It's where you don't get offered anything unless we're desperate. You get on it if you pull some bullshit at a job or you don't turn up or whatever. This guy Timothy was on it, don't know why. The new job came in, we didn't have anyone to fill it. We asked him. Think he'd been out of work for a few weeks; he said yes. He said that he would take the job. It's quite far away, out by the ring road. There's not really a bus that goes up there as such. It's about a mile from the bus stop. It's up by where there's a little shopping centre there. That's where you get off the bus. You walk up and cross the ring road and it's one of those prefab warehouse buildings with an office in the back. The job was in the office. Filing and that. Photocopying. The first guy we got in to do it was Timothy something, can't remember his surname. It was a hard one to get people to do because of the location, because the warehouse is out on the ring road, or near the ring road. Nobody on our books really lives out there. The buses don't go out that near it. Everyone wants to work in the centre of town these days. This guy Timothy phones me on his first day and tells me that he's sat there with no work to do. Something like that. It was quite loud on his end, you could hear the machinery there in the background. I told him to sit tight, something like that. Next day he phones me again and says the same thing. There are some women in the office, they don't have anything for him to do. He doesn't have a computer logon and the computer guy is off sick. The manager who made the booking for a temp isn't in either. He tells me he's just sitting there. I tell him I'll try to see what's going on. I phone the manager but he's not in. I get one of the women in the office telling me he's not in and she doesn't know when he'll be back. She's a nice woman that woman. I've spoken to her on the phone quite a bit. Lives out by the ring road, I think, on one of the estates there. She's in her fifties, I think. The guy, this Timothy guy, took the Friday off, called in sick, which is never a good sign. He's done this kind of thing before. I said to Claire in the office, I said to her that he wouldn't be back. He phoned in on the Monday and said he wasn't going in again. Said he couldn't go somewhere with no work to do. I told him how stupid he was being and that it was going to be difficult for us to look for any more work for him now that he was turning down perfectly good jobs. Whatever. So that was on a Monday morning and we needed to find someone else to get there. I called up this guy called John, think his surname was Cherry. John Cherry that would have made him. Haha. Ha. Hahaha. John Cherry. That is a funny name. I think it really was John Cherry. Ha. This guy, haha, John Cherry. He was new on the books. I think I had interviewed him the previous week. He had been out of university six months without having a job. Wait wait. Ahahahaha. Cherry. OK, OK. Sorry. OK. Ha. OK. Ha. OK. OK. So, um, ha, he went in the same day. I think he got there at about one in the afternoon. He lived right on the other side of town, but I made it clear that he should go in that day. It takes a long time to get out there because it's by the ring road. It's hard to get there, I think, no buses really go up that way. He phoned me from there the next day, the next morning, I think it was. He said he'd got there about one the previous afternoon, on the Monday, but there hadn't been anything for him to do. He couldn't get a computer login because the computer guy was on long-term sick with stress and the manager was on holiday. He said there were some OK women there in the office but they all had jobs to be getting on with and they couldn't really give him anything to do, especially since he didn't have a computer logon, login. Is it login or logon? Login . . . Login. Anyway. Logon. Anyway. He lasted a week there. He called me up every day more and more irritated, the computer guy was still off with stress and the manager was still on holiday. By the Friday he said he wasn't prepared to go back in on the Monday unless there would be something for him to do. I told him, I said to him, he wasn't in a position to be making those kind of demands. I got the impression he was about to back down when I said to him what it is is you are lucky to have a job at all. Fuck you, he said to me. That's what he said to me! I couldn't believe it. I went round to all the guys in the office after the call and told them about it. I was about to tell John Cherry on the phone about that we weren't prepared to put up with unappreciative people like him, but he hung up on me. Then I went round to all the guys in the office and told them about what he said to me. So it was Friday, about half three, and I had to find a replacement for this guy John Cherry. I had wanted to leave at four that day but I was stuck making calls until more like half past. I found this girl Chloe who said she would do it, then first thing Monday morning she phones up and says she's done some research on the company on the internet and she doesn't want to work for them for ethical reasons. I couldn't understand what her problem was. I asked her exactly what the problem was and she went through it in some detail, but I still couldn't really understand it. Look, I said to her, I distinctly remember saying this to her, Look, I said, when you want to have a job you have to be prepared to make certain sacrifices. Everybody needs a job, I told her. But she was having none of it. So that Monday not only did I have all the post to open but I also had to fill this job again. It was a nightmare. It was. It was a bloody nightmare. I can't believe how people can be so ungrateful. Nobody was biting on that Monday, so I had to call up the office and tell them that it might be another day or so. The manager was on holiday so I spoke to a nice woman there. They are a lovely bunch in that office, that's what I tell anyone I send there. They are nice. They are a nice bunch. So on Tuesday I managed to get another girl – Zoe, I think her name was – she was reluctant at first because she would have to get two buses out there in the mornings, so she would be spending over two hours travelling every day. I told her they were a lovely bunch in that office and she eventually accepted. She got there on the Wednesday morning. I remember it was a really wet day that day. On the Thursday she called me to say that there was nothing to do, everyone was being nice to her and they had shown her round the office and everything, but they were all busy with their own work and that she couldn't do anything because she didn't have a computer login. I think it is login. The IT guy was on long term sick because of stress and he was the only one who could give people logins. It was against their company policy for her to use someone else's logon. See, now I think it's logon. Also the manager, the guy who made the booking with us, was on holiday, and it was really his job to delegate to the other employees what to do, so the women in the office couldn't really tell Zoe what she should be doing. They didn't know exactly what the manager wanted her to do either. She worked the Friday, but she left halfway through Monday. She called me on the bus home from her mobile and said it was too boring to work there. She even told me that since she had a chemistry degree she felt she would like to be doing something more along the lines of what she had studied. I told her how naive she was being, but in reality it was too late anyway, you can't just walk out of a job halfway through the day and expect us to be willing to employ you again straight away. Besides, we didn't have any jobs in that needed a chemistry graduate. So anyway the job needed filling again. At first I thought I got lucky, the first guy I called, this guy called Will, he said he would do it, sounded really enthusiastic actually. I was all ready for him to start on the Tuesday, but he called me up early in the morning and said he'd had a better offer from another agency for a job in the centre of town, one that paid better and one that had some crossover with his overall career plan. For the first thing, I told him, we don't encourage people who register with us to join other agencies, it's against our policy, so we wouldn't be able to offer him another job in the future. I told him that equally it was unprofessional to accept a job and then turn it down. Do you know what he said to me? He told me that he couldn't care less and hung up the phone. The cheek! I don't think people realise how hard we have to work and how difficult our jobs are. And then to make matters worse, I got an email from the manager of that job, he had taken time out from his holiday to send an email to me saying that he was disappointed with the high turnover of staff and with how little had been done by the staff I had sent. He also cced the email to my manager, which was inconvenient. Fortunately I'd been liaising regularly with her and she understood the details of the situation. Still, it looked bad. And with this Will guy dropping out and everything else there had been several days where the position had not been filled. So I spent the rest of the day calling round and eventually I got this woman Joan to agree to start the next morning. Originally she had wanted to wait till the Thursday to go in because her daughter was in hospital having a baby, but I managed to talk her round by saying that we really couldn't wait any longer to get anyone in, they were desperate and if she couldn't do it I would have to ask someone else. So she went in. I didn't hear anything from her for the first couple of days, which was a good sign. She was an older lady, about fifty maybe. She had registered with us after being made redundant by this company she had worked for for twenty years. I hoped she was getting on with the women in the office. I'd told her what a lovely bunch they are on the phone, so. But then on the Monday she phoned me and told me that so far she hadn't been given anything to do, that she wasn't able to get a login, the manager and the computer guy were both away. I told her to sit tight and wait and eventually something would come up, that's kind of a standard piece of advice that I give in this kind of situation. But, right, she said to me that I had told her the company were desperate to get someone in. I told her about the email that the manager had sent me from on his holidays, taking time out of his own private time to express concern and also that just because the company were desperate to get someone in, that didn't mean that there was going to be anything exciting for them to do. It's work after all, I told her, you don't go to work and expect to be excited. Go to the cinema if you want that. But unfortunately you can't make a living out of going to the cinema, I told her, so you have to go to work. You might not enjoy it, but you're not the only one, everyone has to do it so you might as well put up with it instead of thinking that you're special. She seemed all right with that, though still quite angry. Then about half an hour later one of the women from the office, a lovely woman, I think she was called Jenny, she called up and said that this Joan was a bit of a trouble-causer, she, Joan that is, not this Jenny, she was going round the office asking what work people were doing and if there was any she could do, asking if she could use other people's logons, asking where the manager was, asking what was wrong with the IT guy, the computer guy, and she had upset one of the other ladies, a lovely lady called Daniele, by saying that it was unscrupulous of the manager to hire someone and then go away without leaving instructions. Daniele, quite rightly, didn't like hearing that about a man she had a lot of respect for and a good relationship with. So I phoned up Joan at the office and told her that the kind of arrogance that she was displaying didn't sit right with what the agency is about, that there is a certain decorum that we expect from employees when they're in the workplace. Now, what you get up to in your own time, that's your business. That's not our business. What you get up to in your own time can be whatever you want it to be. We neither condone nor condemn it. We take no interest, as long as it doesn't affect your performance at your work assignment. That's what we tell everyone who signs up with us, as long as it doesn't affect your performance at work, it doesn't matter what you do in your spare time. Do whatever you want as long as you turn up for work on a Monday morning. Your weekend could be as mad as you like, we don't care, as long as on Monday morning you're there bright and early and ready for the week ahead. You could have been out all weekend, getting pissed, getting leathered, we don't make any moral judgement. The only time we make a judgement like that is if you don't turn up for work on a Monday morning, or you turn up late or unprepared for the week ahead. That's the only time when we would make a judgement. Come five on a Friday, you're free to get up to whatever it is that you want to get up to. We're not going to question you on that. We're not going to call you up and ask how you spend your Saturday nights. We're not going to ask what you get up to of a Sunday. You might go to church, for all we know! But we don't want to know. We don't need to know. You might be there, pally with a priest, you might say confession. You might go out on a Friday and then confess it all to a priest on a Sunday. What you say to a priest, that's not really our business. That's between you and the priest. We don't get involved in what goes on between you and a priest. Or if you have a dog, we don't concern ourselves with if you have a dog or not. Unless for example your dog gets sick and you need to take it to the vet one day instead of going to work. Then we would be very interested in why you were missing work, whether there wasn't someone else who could take the dog to the vet for you so that you could go into work, whether what was wrong with the dog was serious enough to warrant the dog going to the vet at all, or whether perhaps it could perhaps wait till the weekend. If it could wait till the weekend then we don't need to know about it. It's only things that affect whether you can turn up to work on time, ready to go, those are the things we care about. Anything else, it's up to you. Anything you do when it doesn't involve us, that's fine, that's not a problem. What it is is that there can be a problem when what you do in your own time affects what happens when you're in the workplace. Our job, the job of Recruitment Consultant, is to make sure, partly it's to make sure that what you do in your own time stays in your own time and what you do when you're at work conforms to the standards set out by your employer who is both us and the person you're actually working for. What it is is we get people to come into the office, we talk to them and then we decide what job they might be good at and then we put them in a job. And well, sometimes they are OK, other times they are not OK. The main thing is that they turn up for work when they're meant to, wearing what they've been told to wear and do whatever they get told to do. The worst thing is when people don't even do that. The worst thing for us is when someone is ungrateful about all the hard work we've put in on their behalf. I can't, you know, I can't believe the amount of rude people we get. We had a guy in a couple of weeks ago and he was in a call centre job, a nice little job, lovely bunch of people in that office, and what it was was that you have to get your timesheet signed by your line manager and faxed over to us by four o'clock on a Friday. If you don't do that then we can't process the timesheet and you can't get paid until the following week. Anyway this guy was working in a call centre and he called us up and said – it wasn't me he spoke to actually, it was Gemma, do you know Gemma? – he said to Gemma that part of his job was that he wasn't allowed to not be manning the phones at any time, that was expressly a fundamental rule of his job. He said that since he had to be manning the phones at all times, particularly at the key time of between three and five-thirty which is when people start arriving home from picking kids up at school and work so they are stressed enough to be susceptible to calls, since because of all that he couldn't just get up and get his line manager, who was also incidentally a very busy man particularly at that peak time, to sign his timesheet and then take the time to go to the fax machine and take time faxing it to us. That wasn't practical. It also wasn't practical for him to get it signed for the whole week and faxed at lunchtime during his break because what if he got it signed and faxed and then just walked off? He would be getting paid for hours that he hadn't worked. He could be getting as much as four hours of pay for no work. That's as much as twenty-five pounds that the company would be out of pocket. Something like that just wasn't an acceptable solution. Anyway this guy, I think his name was Dan, he calls up Gemma – do you know Gemma? – and tells her all this and says that, well, he has to get paid because otherwise he won't be able to afford his rent, how will he buy food, all these kinds of things. And Gemma had to say to him, like I would have said him, look, what happens in your spare time, that stuff about rent and bills and food, we don't concern ourselves with it. It swings both ways, she told him, and I would have told him the same, whatever it is that you want to get up to on a Saturday night that's fine by us, we're not going to ask about it. But you can't turn round to us and tell us that you have problems paying your rent then. It's not our responsibility to work out your finances for you. It's not our responsibility to see that you have the money to go out on a Friday night, it's up to you to manage your own finances. If you miss the deadline for handing in a timesheet we can't guarantee that we'll pay you the following Friday. We tell people that in advance to stop these kinds of complaints, but do they stop? No. This guy was on to Gemma for at least half an hour, just going on at her about it. Saying that the time he took for this phone call was longer than it would have taken for him to stop phoning people and get his timesheet and fax it over. Gemma told him, and I would have told him the same, that he was missing the point of the rules of work. The rules of his work are that he has to man the phones at a particular time. Just because that happens to clash with when he's meant to get his timesheet in to us is nothing to do with us, it's up to him to find a solution which suits everyone, not just him. He told Gemma that if we weren't prepared to take the timesheet in half an hour late then he was going to quit his job. He was prepared to quit a job we'd given him over something like that! Gemma told him, and I would have told him the same, that doing so would leave the call centre a man down, would make it difficult for us to consider him for future employment and wouldn't make any difference to when we processed his timesheet. One of the girls in the office, actually she was a temp herself, called Lauren, she said afterwards that we should just put his timesheet through. But Gemma and I both told her that the rules are there for a reason, you can't just go bending them for anyone. Lauren said that we often put timesheets through late for some people, but like Gemma said – do you know Gemma? – those people are people that are friends with Gill, the manager of the agency, or friends with us. It's different in those cases because you know that those are genuine people and their reasons for not getting timesheets in are decent, honest reasons. Like this one woman, Sarah, she is a mate of Gill's and she has had like eight or nine jobs in the past few weeks, she keeps quitting them because they are boring. But you know that because she is a mate of Gill's that when she says boring it's different to someone you don't know saying it, you know what she means when she says boring. When Sarah says boring you have a sense of what she means. I've gone for drinks with her and Gill and she's a good laugh, she doesn't take things too seriously. So like, what was I saying?

Yeah, yeah, so we can put timesheets through for her because we know that when she forgets to send them in on time it's for a good reason, and Gill doesn't want to piss her off anyway because Gill's going out with her ex, I mean Sarah's ex, so she doesn't want to piss her off at all because that's kind of a touchy area actually. So Lauren was wrong in that instance. And the guy did quit from the call centre, which was very unprofessional of him. In fact the manager of the call centre phoned up after the guy had finished on the phone with Gemma, Gill took the call, and he asked her if we could put the timesheet through because the guy was serious about quitting and he was actually quite a decent worker. Gill put him straight. She told him that the rules were there for a reason, and if we were to bend them for one person then everyone would want them bending and that would be an administrative nightmare for the agency. She would rather lose one troublesome worker than have that administrative nightmare on her hands and perhaps the guy running the call centre had the luxury of having enough staff on hand to deal with extra work like that but she certainly didn't and since it was her, not him, that sorted out paying temps and she has been in the job for like two years then if she wants advice on how to pay temps from him using a system that has worked very effectively for two years then she'll ask him rather than him calling her up and calling into question a system that has been in place for over two years and has worked very well, thank you very much. Gill came out after the call and told us all about it, how she had properly put the guy in his place, that it was all right for him just dealing with a few agency workers at his call centre but what about her having to deal with hundreds of them all at different workplaces? What about her having to deal with the administrative nightmare repercussions of letting just anybody put a late timesheet through? What about her having to deal with the phone calls from managers? What about her having to provide statistics to head office on payments? What about her having to speak to head office management on a regular basis and could she just casually tell them that, Oh yeah, we put timesheets through early for some guys for no particular reason, we're just a free and easy branch, we let it all hang out at this branch. Is that what head office management want to hear? Is that how you speak to head office management? As if they don't have enough on their plate without having to hear stuff like that. This is what that guy who phoned up Gemma – do you know Gemma? – this is what that guy who phoned her didn't realise. He seemed to think he was entitled to something without respecting the rules. Unfortunately life doesn't work like that, as Gemma said to him – do you know Gemma? – and I would have said the same thing to the guy. Maybe that's how it works in computer games, maybe in computer games you can go around stealing things, shooting people, taking drugs, badmouthing people, but in real life you have to keep quiet, do as you're told and follow the rules. That's just how you get on in real life. That's what some of these guys don't seem to appreciate. So the guy did quit his job, but like Gill said, and I would have said the same, we were glad because the guy was clearly a troublemaker, he was clearly not someone who took working for us seriously. So anyway what was I saying? Yeah, yeah, so I told all this to this Joan. I called her up and told her that what she gets up to in her own time is none of our business, that type of thing. She actually got quite nasty, what she was saying to me. She said to me that I made her miss the birth of her first granddaughter for nothing. Me personally! I told her, I said to her, that I wasn't prepared to accept that accusation, that just because it happened to be me that she was dealing with didn't mean that I was personally responsible for her. I'm not your mother, I said to her. All I did was give her advice on taking a job, a very nice little job in an office with a lovely bunch of people, and she was right to take it because let's be honest, she is something like fifty, only ever had the one job – I didn't say this to her obviously – she, uh . . . no transferable skills to speak of, very little in the way of positives that we can use as an agency to find her work, to sell her to companies basically. And I told her, I said to her that what it is is that while she made a good decision taking that job, she was making a bad decision causing trouble at it and then speaking to me like this on the phone in a very disrespectful way, making personal accusations. I had to say to her, look. Look, I said to her, you might think you are special, your family might think you are special and to them I'm sure you are special, but to us you're just another employee, we treat you the same as anyone else. It doesn't matter if you're gay, straight, black, white or green, you get the same treatment from us. That's just our policy, if you don't like it you can go elsewhere, but I'd be very surprised if you find another employment agency that will treat you any differently, and I should know, I've been in the business almost six months. Anyway so it became obvious that it just wasn't working with Joan. So I had to call around again to try to find someone to fill the job. I called up quite a few people but nobody was responsive – either they said it was too far out, or the pay was too low, all that kind of thing. Eventually I got in touch with this guy Matthew. This was another guy from on our shitlist. This Matthew had quit jobs we'd given him before, so I was a little reluctant to offer it to him, but he seemed keen and he assured me that he would be conscientious in this new job. So I decided to give him a chance. He was going to start the following Monday, this was Friday that I was calling him. Anyway just then Debbie comes in – do you know Debbie? She's Gill's friend's daughter – and she is looking for work again. Debbie has been registered with us for a while and had been doing bits and pieces for us. Anyway it turns out that Debbie has just moved in to a flat out by the ring road with her boyfriend and she's wondering if there's a job going out there. What a coincidence! So Gill took her into her office and then sent me an email telling me to withdraw the offer we made to Matthew since Debbie was going to take the job. I didn't think it would seem plausible for me to ring him up just a few minutes after I had offered him the job and withdraw it, so I waited till I arrived on the Monday and then called Matthew up with the news. He told me he had already left the house, he was quite rude to me actually. Anyway Debbie phoned in sick that day but she went in on the Tuesday. On Tuesday afternoon I got an email from Gill telling me to phone the office because Debbie hadn't been given any work to do or a computer login. So I phoned up and spoke to Daniele there, who is a lovely lady by the way, the whole bunch of them in that office are lovely, and I asked her what was going on, why Debbie hadn't been given any work to do or a computer logon. She explained to me that the manager who had made the booking, and knew exactly what he wanted the temp to be doing, was on holiday and that unfortunately the man who sorts out all their IT, including computer logins, was off on long-term sick with stress. So there was no way currently that she could get onto the network. I put all this in an email to Gill who took the time to phone them up herself and see what the situation was. They told her pretty much the same as what they had told me, that the boss was away and the IT man was off sick. It turned out that this particular job didn't exactly suit Debbie's needs, and in fact another job had come up which Gill thought she was perfect for in town, so we transferred her to that. I called up Matthew and told him that the job was available again. At first he was quite cagey, he asked a lot of questions about why it hadn't been available for three days all of a sudden and then why it had become available again. I told him that it was our policy not to give out information about bookings except what is pertinent for the temp to know. He said he would take the job and we rang off. Then two minutes later he phones me up again and says, Oh wait, all of a sudden I'm not available any more. I asked him why and he told me that it was his policy not to give out availability information to people like me except for what is pertinent for people like me to know. Can you believe that? I said to Claire in the office afterwards – do you know Claire? – I said to her that that's what happens why you try to give second chances to people that have been shitlisted. I've seen it time and time again. We try to give people opportunities and they throw them back in our faces. They bite the hand that feeds them, they really do. That's a funny expression isn't it? To bite the hand that feeds them, that feeds you. To bite the hand that. It's an odd way of putting it. I hadn't ever really thought about it before, you know? But er ... I can't get my head around why these people register with us and then when we try to do something for them they are so aggressive towards us. If you don't want to work for us then why register with us? That's what I'm forever asking these people. It's the one thing that I can't understand. These people seem to think that going to work is like going into a supermarket or something, you can just pick and choose what you want and that's all fine. But going to work isn't like that, there are certain rules that you have to follow and certain professional courtesies that you have to uphold. If you don't do this then I don't see how you can expect to get a job or stay in a job. If you're in a supermarket you can hop from one aisle to the next, do you know what I mean? One minute you can be picking up cheese, the next you're picking up eggs. Work isn't like that. You have to accept that you're going to be doing the same thing, the same task all day every day, week after week, year after year, and that's if you're lucky enough to have a job that's stable. That's what the lucky ones can expect. This is why I just don't get it when people treat working like it's a pick 'n' mix. What does the 'n' stand for in pick 'n' mix? Like you can take a little of this and a little of that and expect to be paid for it and have security. It just doesn't work like that. So since Matthew wasn't doing it I had to find someone else. I started phoning around again. A lot of people I spoke to were reluctant about taking the job. It is fairly low pay and the location is inconvenient – it's out by the ring road, you know – but I just don't see how these people can be so fussy – not taking a reasonable job offer is a mark against you in my book and it makes me less likely to ask you in the future. Then when I don't phone them for a few days they're on to me asking what we've got in, what work is available for them to do. I have to tell them, I say to them that there was a perfectly good job that they turned down and any new jobs that do come in, I'm more likely to ring up people who say yes than people who say no. That's just logical. If people have a record of saying no then eventually I'll stop ringing them altogether, unless I'm desperate. That's something that every Recruitment Consultant does. Why would you continue to ring someone who has said no regularly in the past? You wouldn't. You just don't do it. What would be the point? I don't know what the point of that would be. I just don't think that these guys appreciate all the hard work we put in, ringing round, getting people to go to jobs. We're giving them opportunities. Opportunities that further their careers. They don't seem to appreciate or understand that. They think we have it easy. They think we don't work hard. But they are wrong. It's a hard job. I think it's a misunderstood job. I. I feel hot. Is anyone else hot? Are you hot? Is it warm in here? I feel like I. One thing I. I never felt that . . . It is hot, isn't it? I'm hot. I'm definitely warm. Do you . . . has the music stopped? I. I thought it had stopped then, it's just changing songs. Is . . . Does anyone have an apple? I think I could actually eat an apple. A red apple. Ahahahaha. A red apple. A . . . what CD is this? Is my drink? I . . . have I finished it? I thought the bottle was by the chair. Was it a bottle? Has someone turned that song down? Can someone? I can't . . . Has someone unplugged the stereo? I can't hear it any more. Could someone see if . . . What it is, you know, what it is is that . . . When I look now at what I've done I feel . . . When I see what I've done . . . When I . . . If . . . I . . . Me . . . I . . . I . . .

The bear takes his seat. The auditorium is poky and dilapi-dated. He struggles to make himself comfortable with so little leg room. He sips on his lager. He does all these things in the silence of his own thoughts. It occurs to him to wonder how the others around him think. What is their mechanism for thinking? What is the human mechanism? In vain he asks this question to himself. He looks around at them, mostly groups of young people together sipping their lagers from plastic cups or sipping spirits from smaller plastic cups. Or sipping nothing. He can't make out any of their conversations. He sees some men alone, sitting alone in seats, a few with whole aisles to themselves. On the stage there is a man talking to another man, but it is clear that this is not part of the entertainment. It's hard to think with all the noise of people talking and moving around. A few more men get on stage. People continue to take their seats. A young couple comprising one attractive man and one attractive woman sit down a couple of seats from the bear. The bear admires the woman's hairstyle and the man's trousers. These things he sees. On those people, the hairstyle, the trousers, they appear natural. The bear con-siders his own jeans, with their huge stretch waistband and slack knees. He considers the stiff hair unshorn at the top of his head. It has always been difficult for this bear to be stylish. He has often lamented not being thinner, slighter. It has never been easy for him to find clothes that fit well in colours and styles that appeal. He has a fondness for open-necked shirts, well-tailored dark, almost charcoal, chalk-striped trousers, brightly patterned dashiki, wool jumpers with crisp white shirts and silk ties, leather shoes with Cuban heels, argyle socks, Miles Davis' style in the 1970s, the suits Serge Gainsbourg wore. The bear's reflections are interrupted by some commotion in the back of the auditorium. Two men are helping a third man wearing sunglasses, evidently blind, down the aisle and onto the stage. Once there they hand him a trumpet which he blows a few notes into. Someone comes and whispers into his ear. The man nods. A few people leave the stage. Those remaining take their places and gather up their instruments.

One of the men walks to the front of the stage. He is carrying a bassoon. Ladies and gentlemen, he says, you may be familiar with the term 'free jazz'. For those that use it, it is generally speaking a descriptive term. For us, though, it is an imperative, a direction, an instruction. For we seek to truly free jazz, to free it from the constraints of tradition, of songcraft, of the false certainties of composition, rhythmic coherence and the Western scale. There is a ripple of applause and he returns to the back of the stage. There is a pause. The drummer taps out a short flourish and then hits a crescendo on the largest cymbal. A cymbal is both a cymbal and a machine which amplifies and in that amplification makes plain the sympathetic music of the cosmos. All the remaining instruments pile in with a big burst of noise, all except the blind trumpeter who stands, looking indifferent.

◆

The bear thinks back to the time he attended an adult education class in painting. For his piece he chose to do a lifesize portrait of Keiji Haino. At first they didn't understand. Even the teacher was sceptical. The bear chose a monochrome palette, depicting Haino in a long black coat, leaning heavily on a black cane, his eyes hidden by sunglasses. At Haino's feet, the only part of the painting in colour, is his red telecaster. The bear hears it even now, sending out unremitting, unrelenting, unmitigated, undulating shrieks throughout the universe, even now drawing fire, spitting colour, mimicking a hoarse man gasping his last gasp. In the art class, sure, they had been cynical, but that portrait of the dark magus of avant-rock now hangs over the art room, so brooding, so powerful.

Some of the players are now constructing a low drone over which the guitarist is running spindly lines punctuated by sharp stabs of colour. A guitar is both a guitar and a construction of wood, plastic and metal. A man sitting in front of a laptop screen and banks of wires and boxes is suddenly swept up in a hurry of motion and the fizzing noise from his laptop modulates and stretches out, the sound deepens, running in and out of time with the guitar, adding layers of reverb which crash against each other so that the sound clips and shudders. A laptop is both a laptop and a means of carving the world up into disparate pieces, so as to make its apprehension easier. One of the men gives a low moan into a microphone. The human voice is both the human voice and the instrument we use to curse god, to howl at god for being so far from us. Only the blind trumpeter stands still, not playing.

And the bear thinks back to the time he attended an adult education class in painting. For his piece he decided to do a lifesize portrait of Steven Stapleton. There was some cynicism at first, some disgruntlement among the staff and students of the adult education centre. The project was too ambitious, too ridiculous. But the bear pressed on with it. He chose to portray Stapleton seated in a large ornate throne, covered in skulls, horns and other occult objects. The bear decided that he would do Stapleton's face, beard, shades and top hat in a photorealist style, but as you moved outwards from this focal point the painting would be rendered increasingly abstract, so that at the edges of the picture there were mere floating phantasms of colour, the swirling, effervescent tone-world of Stapleton's unforgiving music. They all said it couldn't be done at the art class, but that portrait of the dark magus of avant-electronics now hangs over the art room, so brooding, so powerful.

The man at the piano is playing heavy tone clusters on the lower-register keys with his left forearm. The piano is both a piano and a node in a dense nexus of musical styles and traditions, both a major part in the history of colonialism and a means by which colonialism can be challenged. Next to him, another man, kneeling down, swaying back and forth, is wailing, high-pitched and from the back of the throat, what sounds like 'too bad' over and over again.

The drummer punctuates the 't' of too and the 'b' of bad in short bursts. The blind trumpeter still does not play. The double-bassist sprinkles plangent ripples across the hall. A double bass is both a double bass and a weapon.

The bear thinks back to the time he attended an adult education class in painting. He decided to do a lifesize portrait of Diamanda Galas at the piano. Galas's head was to be thrown back in anguish, her teeth bared, her hands like claws at the keys. Each key was to be painted with the face of a twentieth-century political dictator. The denizens of the art room were dubious to say the least. They doubted that this bear could pull off such a piece. The bear painted the picture with a muted palette, paying particular attention to Galas's hands. A long red fingernail, with a point of pearlescent white light glinting off it, angles down at the startled face of Mussolini, while Pinochet looks on in distress. The art teacher was uncertain, he was unsure, he speculated that it couldn't be done. But that portrait of the dark magus of avant-goth blues now hangs over the art room, so brooding, so powerful.

The improvisation modulates again so that now the assorted brass instruments, with the exception of the blind trumpeter who continues to stand complacently, blast out an edifice of sound, constantly blurring and thickening. The drummer hits the snare, the guitarist draws feedback from the amp, the lines careen in and out of each other, everyone is trying to play louder than everyone else. Simultaneously they play a few bars of high notes, some phantom of melody, a melody that only wants to be wounded, which slips away like a dog under a hedge, which recalls at once the theme tune of a favoured television show from your youth, a record your dad played during your childhood, the promise of true socialism, any notion of a populist avant-garde, any notion of a truly radical egalitarian architecture, some sense of education that is affordable and accessible to all, any idea of debts being halved, or cancelled, or of money being spread out, of opportunities being there for everyone, of exploitation to cease, any notion of life lived in cooperation rather than competition; this melody, it's there, they've done it, it's music.

And the bear thinks back to the time he attended an adult education class in painting. He decided to do a lifesize portrait of Albert Ayler. In the preliminary sketches the bear made for the portrait Ayler's head was tipped back, his back arched, his saxophone raised towards the heavens. The bear chose to depict him in white robes trimmed with silver, Christlike in the darkness. The other people in the class were cynical, they didn't think it could be done. They thought it wouldn't happen. They thought it was an idle boast. They thought it was ridiculous. They thought it was asinine. But they couldn't have been more wrong. They could not have got it more wrong. The bear's Ayler, in the finished portrait, had a saintly posture. His saxophone glowed gold. His eyes were full of the pain of death and the majesty of life and flowing with music. Beads of sweat hung on Ayler's cheeks; spirits, ghosts, spectres clung to him, holding on to the flow of music, the depths of music, flowing out of the darkness, bigger than jazz, greater than death, breathless, erotic, hopeful, the perfect echo of it reverberating around the universe. The art class guys, they weren't positive about the prospects for this project, they banked on failure. But that portrait of the dark magus of avant-jazz now hangs over the art room, so brooding, so powerful.

The horns fall away now, leaving just sparse clusters of piano notes, the same three chords played over and over, slower and slower. The other musicians stand silently. For some time, this goes on. Now the blind trumpeter puts his instrument to his lips. There are gaps of about a minute between each depression of the pianist's hand. It is silent for a time. The other players stand poised with their various instruments. The trumpeter looks doleful. His mouth is turned down. He plays. He begins to play the melody from 'St James Infirmary'. He plays it very slowly. He plays it mournfully. He plays it as a dirge. He completes the melody and brings the trumpet from his lips. He steps forward and he sings the song, low and sweet, his whole body quavering. As he completes the lyric and brings the trumpet once more to his mouth to play the solo, the bear, impossibly moved, stands up, tears in his eyes, and applauds. Just as he stands, just at that moment, just as he stands, the rest of the band break in as one. Other people, those in the audience, some of them turn to look at the bear, but he stays standing. The band do not appear to notice. The band continue to play the song, and play it and play it.

The Recruitment Consultant got home after work. She went into the kitchen. Above the pile of washing-up there was a note which said: You need to do your washing-up because otherwise I won't be able to eat. Thanks – Richard. She went into the living room. Richard was sitting on the sofa watching TV. She looked at him. She knew that he knew she had seen the note. He didn't say anything to her. She went to her room for paper. Silently, she wrote notes about everything that Richard did not do. This is your jumper that you did not pick up. You left this book open and broke the spine. You did not hoover properly here. She stuck the notes in the relevant places. Richard looked at her. She went to do the washing-up.

The bear is at his art class. This term they are doing sculptures. In the first class the teacher had picked a pupil, a woman called Kim, and they all have to do a sculpture of her head. Kim is in the corner, on the far side of the room. The bear looks over at her. She is sculpting her own version of her head, an abstract piece made up of found objects which she is now steadily spraying with neon pink aerosol paint. Arthur, a man in his eighties, is rolling clay into small sausage shapes and sticking them to a larger ball from which protrude several slender wooden sticks. Arthur's Kim looks diseased, with uneven patches of skin and a drooping nose. Hetty, a middle-aged woman, has made a wire frame in the shape of Kim's head and she is now applying papier-mâché to the frame in long gluey strips. Her Kim, with its still open skull, looks forlorn. John, an energetic man in his thirties, is carefully filing away at a large block of wood. He is working on the nose. He wears a mask to keep the sawdust out of his lungs and `it makes him look like a surgeon. His Kim, though still only partially formed, has a proud countenance and seems self-assured. The bear's own effort is to be a kinetic sculpture. A screen shows video footage that he has taken of the sun going down on a beach/a corner shop/the view from a bus window driving through the city on a rainy evening. Behind the screen, two appendages, powered by a small motor, will spin. One holds a torn green dress on a hanger and the other a perspex box filled with coloured jelly beans. The bear looks over at Kim. Her hands move. Under Kim's long skirt, the bear can perceive the musculature of her upper thighs. Her shoulders are heavy and broad. She wears a long skirt and a blouse. Over that she has on an apron which is splattered with bright pink paint. Her face, which the bear seeks to represent with the video, the dress and the jelly beans in combination, is inscrutable in its concentration. Kim looks dead hard at her assortment of pink tins, bits of pink plastic and pink metal. The materials have undergone such a transformation in the process of her sorting them and painting them that the bear feels his eyes growing damp. He is moved. Kim's face is made of wire and newspaper. Kim's face is clay and lumpen. Kim's face is hewn from sawdust on the floor. Kim's face is pale and chalky and she has freckles and she has a protruding chin. Kim's face is a screen showing tins of sweetcorn. The bear is gluing together a wooden frame to go around the screen. Kim's face is turned away from him. Furthermore, Kim's face is an empty pink tin which represents both her mouth and her womb in all their abjection and wonder. Moreover, it is a spear of pink plastic, it is a pink Coke bottle, it is a pink cushion.

– Remember that episode which had – it was a really good episode – it had that guy who cooked like the whole side of a cow? And in his house he had all those pictures of fields of cattle stored in his underwear drawer like they were like porn or something.

– That was the guy who dressed like a cowboy?

– Him, yeah. And there was that woman that week and she kept muttering and just laughing to herself, remember?

– Haha, yeah. And she cooked soup for all three courses? Who has ever even had a sweet dessert soup before?

– She kept going on about how everyone else's food contained too much eggs. I don't think they should show stuff like that, it's cruel.

– It's horrible.

– It's exploitative. Imagine seeing that and if it was yourself.

– She was weird though, she dressed like an old woman even though she wasn't an old woman. She was actually probably like my age or –

– The cowboy one really seemed to fancy her though. He gave her his cowboy hat and –

– I don't remember that. Did he? Did he give her his cowboy hat?

– He gave her his cowboy hat and he said that he admired her soups. He got quite drunk and said in the taxi that he thought she had good flanks or something like that. Still only gave her a seven though.

– I don't get that, when they rave about people then only give them like a seven.

– Remember that woman who gave everyone a four and then she had to go back and change all her votes? Because she was cheating.

– I don't think I saw that one.

– Basically, even, however good the meal was that the person served she only gave them a four so that she would win. But they made her redo all the marks and, well, she still won but by less overall points.

The bear is sitting in between two women who are having this above conversation. He does like the show that they are talking about. He finds it difficult, though, to find an appropriate caesura in the conversation in which to make a comment himself. One of the women will start talking just as the other is finishing the last syllable of her sentence. Their almost encyclopaedic knowledge of the show is another barrier to joining in. They lean slightly forward on the sofa to see each other better, while the bear leans back to better allow them to see each other. The bear sips his drink. Unnoticed by anyone else, the white cat is sitting on the rug masturbating. Her head turns to the bear and she looks brazenly at him. Groups of people chatter. In another room someone slurs along with a chorus of saccharine, glorious disco. The bear feels like getting up and maybe dancing.

– Remember that one guy's house that had all the snakes? I wouldn't want to go into a house like that.

– Do you not like snakes?

– No. No, I like snakes. I mean I get claustrophobic. His house was really poky. I don't like houses like that. He had too much stuff in it. Too much junk and that.

– I know what you mean.

– There was that one woman on it and she really reminded me of Carol.

– Carol that's here Carol, you mean, or another Carol?

– No, Carol that's here. She had like the same kind of, uh, demeanour, she had a similar haircut.

– Which one was that on, I don't think I've seen it?

– It was the one with, ah, I think she cooked pheasant compote with a rich pink peppercorn jus served in a ramekin. I think it was served with an asparagus, petit pois and cloves purée.

– O yeah, I think I recall this episode. And she was stressing because the compote didn't exactly turn out perfect. I think it was that there was some charring or something on the top of the compote. Is that what you do with a compote? Anyway the way she was stressing reminded me of Carol so.

– I get that. I think I might have seen that one. Did she serve ape fingers wrapped in ham, parmesan and breadcrumbs as a starter?

– No, I think she served baked avocado stuffed with quail's egg and a honey/mustard jus.

– Oh right, because, ah, the woman who did the fingers had a haircut that was like Carol's.

– I don't think I've seen that one. What was the main course?

– Braised bream and monkfish with a rich shallot gravy

served with savoury macaroons and the macaroons were stuffed with gruyere, truffle oil and minced pork.

The disco is still continuing. It sounds like hot air balloons rising over an Arctic tundra. It sounds like rain over the ocean. The cat is still masturbating on the rug. It sounds like the pyramids rising over hills in the heat haze. Some woman is singing on it. It sounds like light refracted through crystal, throwing blurry miniature rainbows all over the room. The bear wants to get up and dance but he feels ensnared by the cat and the conversation. There still hasn't been an opportunity for him to speak and he feels now that it has been too long, that anything he might say would seem odd, trivial, banal, like he was trying to inter-rupt. He sips on his drink, which is nearly empty. There is, though, another can near to his feet. The cat looks at the bear. The bear is unhappy about the animal's brazenness, its willingness to take its pleasure in the rooms of men. To lie in front of them and show them clearly what it is. That confidence, that blind animal indifference, this this bear envies. The cat looks up at him with calm, intent eyes. Still, though, the appearance of self-mastery often conceals a deeper weakness. It sounds like a river just beginning its yawning trickle down a mountain and at the same time minutely shaping the mountain in all its majesty.

– I don't think I would go on that show really, no. You always end up looking like an idiot if you go on it, I think.
– I don't know, I think I would go on it. I think I would, yeah.

– I bet they edit people to look more stupid than they are. Or they just pick a lot of stupid people to go on it.

– They just pick stupid people to go on it, I think. And then they edit them also to look stupid. I would go on it still. I'd like to go round people's houses and meet people and that.

– What would you cook on it if you went on it?

– I would probably . . . did you see that one who hollowed out a whole loaf of bread and he cooked rats in it?

– Nah.

– Well, I like the idea of hollowing out a whole loaf of bread and then what I would do is chew up the cut-out bread in my cheeks until it formed a paste and then put that back into the hollowed out intact bread along with jarlsberg, crème-fraiche, halloumi, gruyere, mozzarella, Greek yoghurt, cheddar, goat's cheese, feta cheese, cottage cheese, stilton and Monterey Jack. I would then bake the whole thing and serve it with a cheese board.

– Mmmm. Mmmmmmm. That sounds a-ma-zing. That sounds really, really nice. Mmmm.

– Yeah, so what would you cook if you were on it?

– Well, like I say, I wouldn't go on it, I don't think, but if someone put a gun to my head – not that they would, I hope! – I would probably make . . . have you ever had chinchilla meat?

– Hm, I don't think I have? I've had shrew and I've had weasel though.

– Mmm, weasel is so good. I've never eaten shrew, what is it like?

– It's reminiscent of stoat. I've only had it the once, it was served in a Chinese-style rich red wine gravy with wasabi and soy sauce with snakeskin croutons.

– God, I love snakeskin croutons – so crunchy! What was I saying? Yeah, chinchilla, yeah, I would cook that. Chinchilla stuffed with ginger, shallots, fennel and pistachios. Served with asparagus in a béchamel, cloves and liver sausage sauce.

– Mmmmm!

The bear looks askance at the two women. To him, this food they are describing does not sound at all palatable. The cat, on the rug, has finished and now lies in its somnolence, still gazing at the bear, who cracks open his last can. The bear looks at the cat, the cat looks at the bear. In the other room, the disco has given way to strident psychedelia sung in Turkish. The bear hears laughter. He feels as if he wants to get up, but that it's been too long since he's said anything and it may appear rude. The cat still stares. The bear feels dreadfully hot. The curtains are drawn in the room. The song is stunning. It sounds like liberation. The bear's shoes feel tight. It is extremely difficult for him to find appropriate shoes. The cat now rises, stalks across to the bear and jumps up onto his lap. For a second the room is darkened, a moth flies into the lampshade and then out again. Still the cat looks at the bear. The bear puts his paw on the cat's head. He considers how simple it would be for him to crush this cat's head entirely.

– I think there was an episode where there was a woman that served bat. Did you see that one?

– I don't think I saw that one.

– Apparently it tastes a little like beaver. The wings are quite chewy. You can give them to dogs in the same manner you would give a dog a pig's ear.

– Oh right, OK.

– This woman made fricasseed bat served with whole raw giant white onions in their skins.

– I did see that one actually, I think. I was getting it confused with the woman who actually did make beaver.

– That was unfortunate. Everyone enjoyed her beaver, but the rich endive chutney with cottage cheese she served with it lost her points.

– Everyone enjoyed her beaver! Ahahahahhahaha.

– Ahahaha.

– Hahaha ahahaha.

– Hahahaha hahaha.

– Ahahah ahahahaaa.

– It's . . . haha. Ahaha.

– Hahahahaha.

The room is full of dog-headed men. The women's laughter runs through the room. The music sounds like freedom, like emancipation. Some guy shouts something into his mobile. The moth flies into the light again. The cat's claws dig through the bear's jeans into his legs. Still, it purrs. The bear tries to lift the cat off him, but the claws are snagged. The music sounds like a boat on a river. It sounds like a car on a road. Yes, that way, it sounds. It sounds like going over a ridge. It sounds like going under the sky. It sounds like wonder, like beneficence. Someone coughs. People are talking. People are laughing. This room, full of dog-headed men, dog-headed women, full of laughter, full of music. The bear has developed a nasty habit of looking at people and thinking about their money. He looks at this guy in the room. He thinks about this guy's money. Where does he get it?

– Aaaahahahaha.

– Hahaha.

– Ahahahahahaha.

– Aaahahahaaa.

– Hahahahaa.

– Ahah.

– Ha.

– Hahaha wait wait hahahaa.

– Hahahaahahaa.

– Ahahhahahaha.

The bear looks at this guy in the room. How does he do it, this guy? How does he do it? The clothes he is wearing, where did he get the money for them? Did he work for it or was it given to him? Does he work? How did he get into the industry he is in? Who does he know? What does his dad do? What kind of car does his dad drive? This guy, is he thinking now about if he's hungover tomorrow then that's tomorrow wasted and then it's Monday and back to work? Does he need to think about things like that? Is he thinking, if I stay much later then I'll miss the last bus and have to pay for a taxi and how much will that cost from here to home? Is he thinking that? This bear looks at this guy, looks at his hairstyle, the drink he is holding, the mobile phone he takes out of his pocket and glances at, all these things this bear sees. All these things he considers. The bear considers what the combined cost, in money, of the party is, every conceivable cost: the cost of rent for the house they are in for the period of this party, the cost of the electricity that will be used, the cost of the water that will be used or consumed, the resultant cost of the hastening of repair work as a result of the increased usage of electrical wires and water and waste pipes, the cost of all the snacks available at the party, the cost of packaging those snacks, the cost of paying graphic designers to design the packaging for those snacks, the cost of gathering together the ingredients for those snacks including the materials needed for the packaging, the cost of growing those ingredients, the cost of the salaries of the people who work in the factories where those snacks are created, the cost of maintaining those factories, the cost of council tax for the period of the party, the cost of hastened need to replace soft furnishings or repaint walls or replace carpets and other furniture as a result of spills and wear and tear, the cost of the drugs that are being consumed, the cost of the drinks that are being consumed including their manufacture, the growing of the ingredients in them and the cost of manufacturing the packaging in which they come, the cost of the clothes that people are wearing, the cost of the items they have on them including electrical items such as mobile phones and all the attendant manufacturing and distribution costs of these including the cost of maintaining a working mobile phone grid, the costs of all the haircuts, all the makeup, all the nail polish, all the deodorant, all the aftershave, all the perfume, the cost of wear and tear and potential damage to clothes and shoes as a result of moving around the party, the cost of future health care, dental work and or time lost from work as a result of adverse health partially or entirely stemming from this party, the cost of cigarettes smoked at the party and the attendant cost of damage caused to paintwork by cigarette smoke or burns burned into furniture by cigarettes as well as the cost of repairing lungs and throats and teeth as a result of smoking, the cost of any phonecalls made from the party, the cost of transport both to and from the party, the cost of time lost while at the party which could have been spent more lucratively, the cost of all the jewellery worn, including the transport and manufacturing costs of the jewellery, the cost to neighbours of any loss of sleep or discomfort as a result of excessive noise from the party, the cost of the music played including the cost of manufacturing and distributing the media upon which the music was recorded and also the cost of creating the music itself including the cost of the instruments or equipment used by the musicians, the cost of studio time, the cost of marketing, the cost of time lost on subsequent days to hangovers and comedowns, the cost of cleaning products and time necessary to clean the house after the party as well as the manufacture and distribution mechanisms involved in creating and selling those cleaning products, the cost of the maintenance of a nation in which such a party is possible, the cost of the necessity for markets where illegal drugs are sold and all the attendant costs of the manufacture and distribution of those drugs, the cost of balancing or offsetting the carbon emissions from the transport used to travel both to and from the party, the cost of the production of the sort of people who have parties of this sort, the cost of their educations and all their lives which have lead exactly, inevitably, to this particular point in history. The bear tries to estimate what this cost would be, but can get no more accurate than thinking it to be in the tens of billions, possibly hundreds of billions of any currency. The bear wonders if, given that exorbitant cost, the party is worthwhile. The women on each side of him continue to laugh, they are unable to stop laughing. The bears stands up, finally, and goes to get in the queue for the toilet.

The Recruitment Consultant was walking to the bus stop. She had been shopping after work and she was carrying a carrier bag with a brown skirt in it. The skirt was cut just above the knee. It was a Friday and she was thinking about the weekend. It was nice to be out of work. The main road was pretty crowded so she turned off to walk down a side street full of office buildings. She noticed that one of them was a place she recruited for, mostly for call centre work. Out of the corner of her eye, coming down the steps of the building, she noticed one of her temps, a guy she had put into the call centre quite recently. He must have been coming out of work. He looked a little dishevelled, he really should be tidier for work. He was walking ahead of her. He turned away and she continued on, crossing over the road, towards the bus stop.

♠

When she got there, she was surprised to see him already waiting at the stop, headphones in his ears, not noticing her but staring at the road the bus would come down. She had never noticed him at the stop before and in fact recalled from his registration details that he lived on the opposite side of town. Perhaps he had moved. He should really know to update the agency with any change in details. His pay-slips would probably be being sent to the wrong address now. She considered going up to him and having a word, but then chastised herself for thinking too much about work when it was the weekend. The bus came and the long queue slowly filed on to it. By the time the Recruitment Consultant got on, there was only one seat upstairs and that was behind this guy, the call centre guy. She sat down. The bus pulled away. They turned onto the main road and the bus got stuck in the rush hour traffic. They crawled along. The call centre guy's mobile rang and he answered it: All right? Yeah (...) Yeah (...) No, it's bullshit (...) Yeah, I have to ring people up and threaten them with bailiffs or court action. Mostly old people who don't know what's going on and I basically have to intimidate them into paying us (...) What? (...) O, no, I just read it from a script mostly. I just tell them what they owe and how to pay it (...) Yeah, mostly they want to pay when I call and I just transfer them through to some other person who takes payments (...) Right (...) Uh, yeah, well it's just depressing. I keep filling in applications for jobs I don't even particularly want. If I could afford to quit then I would (...) No, no (...) No, not very much – I feel like I'm sitting there and the company shareholders are making loads of money and the agency are making loads of money and the ones losing out are the poor people or old people who have to pay and me who has to sit there for a few quid an hour (. . .) and they even take time off for your fucking toilet breaks (. . .) Exactly (. . .) What? (. . .) Oh, all right, I'll call you later then (. . .) Yeah (. . .) Yeah, bye. Bye. He put the phone back into his pocket and put his earphones in again. The Recruitment Consultant looked out of the window. They were out of town now and moving a little faster in the traffic.

As they approached the Recruitment Consultant's street, she was surprised to see the guy get up just a moment before she did and head down the stairs. She followed and the bus pulled in. They both got off and he, without looking at her, apparently without having seen her at all, walked off in the direction of the Recruitment Consultant's house. She followed a little behind, entirely bemused at the coincidence. He crossed the dual carriageway where she always crossed it, and he took the shortcut across the grass on the corner that she always took. Every turn she was about to make he anticipated and turned before her. The Recruitment Consultant felt thirsty, so when they reached the little row of shops near to her house she decided to go in, she thought this would be a good way of getting rid of the guy as well, except he turned into the same newsagent she always went to. When she went in the door he was already paying for a can of Coke. She picked up a can of Coke and paid for it. He had already crossed the road when she got outside and she crossed it. He then nonchalantly turned into her driveway, fished a set of keys from his pocket and let himself into her house. She stopped. Something wasn't right. She looked all around her and the street that had been so familiar seconds ago now appeared alien to her. This street, it wasn't her street. This house, it wasn't her house. She had no notion of where she was and no idea how to get back to the bus stop. She looked up and down the street. It was a simple row of terraces with some shops on one side of the road. She resolved to knock on the call centre guy's door and ask him for directions. But then, as she took half a step forward, she checked herself – how would that look? She stuck her hands in her pockets and again surveyed the street. She couldn't even recall which direction they had come from. She stood still and thought about what to do. Just then the front door of the house opened again and the call centre guy walked out looking angry. What are you doing here? he shouted. Why have you followed me here? Haven't you got enough of me already? Don't you take enough from me already? He was striding towards her, his face was flushed and his fists were clenched. The Recruitment Consultant stepped backwards in alarm and in alarm she tripped at the kerb, fell and hit her head on the hard tarmac. The call centre guy was alarmed too, and he ran back into his house. When the ambulance finally came it was agreed that the initial impact of the blow to the head had killed her almost instantly. It was the way she fell.

The bear is at work. At his computer, his mouth fills with saliva. He feels a sudden urge to vomit. Carefully, gently, he rises from his chair, his paws on the lip of the desk, pushing his bulk to a standing position. He looks around. His eyes are damp. Under his trousers and shirt he is sweating. It is 11:29. He walks to the door. His throat feels tight, his cheeks feel so warm. He walks down the corridor. In the toilets, there is someone in the next cubicle. So the bear waits, hands braced against the cold cubicle sides. Saliva rises into his mouth and he lets a string of it flow from his tongue and into the toilet bowl. He can hear the sound of the man pissing in the next cubicle. And flushing. The floor of the toilets is flooded with water. The bear hears the noise of the man drying his hands under the electric dryer. The dryer whirs on and off. After a time the man leaves. The bear's whole frame is leant against the cold side of the cubicle. He kneels. The water on the floor soaks into the front of his trousers. It feels OK. The bear leans heavily against the toilet. After a few false starts in his throat he vomits a frothy liquid which falls and sits on the top of the toilet water. He does it again. Several times he vomits, until there is only a thick saliva-like liquid coming up, which makes his teeth furry and tastes heavy, gelatinous. He retches. When that subsides he stands. His eyes are watering. He goes to the mirror. His eyes are red, his skin is dark pink, his teeth are dark yellow. He looks in the mirror. Everything that is animal about him is in front of him. His trousers are dark grey with the damp, they are heavy with the water that has soaked into them. His back is sweating. The density of these details even, they do not convey his sickness. He is not sure how he can go back. Or, if not back, where he can go. With some deliberation he comes to a decision. With some determination he walks back to the office. With some gravitas he picks up his jacket and bag. These are not the actions of someone at work, and nor do they uphold a correct sense of decorum in the workplace. Determination, deliberation, gravitas, they do not belong in the workplace. These are the actions of a free animal. It is not so much the actions themselves, but the manner in which they are completed. It is easy for the bear to forget, in this moment, that there is really no such thing as a real free animal. Even out in the street he is chained to the street. He goes out into the street. He has left another job behind. His tiredness is pronounced. He can feel it in his shoulders.

In the street, he becomes those who do not work. Effortlessly he joins that group. It is a group with its own attendant problems and immediately he takes on board those problems. The problems are: money, how to get it. How can this bear get that money now? He feels the buzz of his mobile phone in his pocket. Looking at the screen he sees it is the agency. He was seen to leave, he was seen going out on the street during work time and not coming back. They will want an explanation. They will not want the explanation this bear has to give. He presses the button and his Recruitment Consultant is on the other end of the phone. Hello, is that Regis? Her voice is flat; gone is all the previous bonhomie, the previous exuberance. She speaks quickly, aggressively. Your line manager Anthony has just been on the phone, he says you've left the office. Is that true? She leaves a beat in which the bear might have begun to speak, but she continues. The thing is, this kind of behaviour isn't acceptable. Are you aware of the agreement you signed when you came to work with us? And not just that,

Anthony was concerned with regard to your whereabouts. You could have been anywhere, OK? As employers we have a duty of care for our staff. How do you think it would look if you had been run over by a bus when you left? If you want to leave a job that's fine but you have to go through the proper procedures, OK? You have to tell us if there's a problem with the job you're in and we'll try to sort it out. We can only help you if you come to us. What did I say at our initial interview? That if you have any grievances with the job then just drop me or one of my colleagues a line, email us or come in in person and we'll try to sort it out, OK? She had managed to master the technique of breathing in the middle of sentences, during words even, so as to be able to continue speaking seamlessly and without interruption. She continued without pause. After this I'm not really sure we're going to be able to work with you any more, OK? You have to understand that this kind of behaviour is unacceptable. If you want to maintain a good relationship with your employer y . . . The bear finally presses the button on his phone to end the call. He puts it back in his pocket. It buzzes again. He takes it out of his pocket. He switches it off.

On top of her now, again, he put his hands on her shoulders and pushes down with his weight, uncomfortably. She wriggles underneath him, trying to shift the weight and he moves his hands down, holding her at the elbows, stretching her out flat. The song begins to skip. Shit, he goes. Shit. He gets off her and goes to the player and skips the song back to the start. She turns over and lies on her side, her forearm over her face. Shuts her eyes. He comes back, hooks his elbow into hers and turns her onto her back again. He pushes into her again. The skin of his stomach pulls her pubic hair, his hip bones beat into her. He licks her neck and she can taste the drink on his breath.

The bear is behind the arras. In front of the arras, which the bear is hiding behind, people are talking about him. Two women are talking about him.

Lisa: What makes you say that?

Carol: I don't know, it's just the way he acts around you.

L: Which is how? You know he ran away the last time he saw me?

C: He ran away?

L: I don't think he knew I'd seen him.

C: That's unbelievable.

L: It's bizarre. He didn't see that I saw him. It was in the supermarket. He actually put his basket full of food down and walked out the shop.

C: This is Regis we're talking about still?

L: Yeah.

C: And what was in his basket?

L: What?

C: What did he have in his basket, the one he put down?

L: Why do you want to know that?

C: I don't know, it just made me think when you said.

L: He had . . . I think he had meat, quite a bit of meat.

C: Just that?

L: Cornflakes maybe? I don't really remember.

Behind the arras, the bear scratches at his chin with his claw. The two women are stood with their backs to him.

C: Anyway, he acts strangely around you.

L: I didn't think he acted any differently around me than he does around you.

C: He does.

L: How so?

C: Well, you know when we worked together?

L: You worked together?

C: He worked at the agency, doing admin, for a couple of weeks. That's where I met him, he temped for us.

L: He never told me that.

C: Well, nor did I. It was a while ago now.

L: Why did he leave?

C: Work?

L: Yeah, why did he have to leave?

C: He didn't have to. He quit. He said he couldn't stand it.

L: How come?

C: That's all he said, he just said that really. Obviously we couldn't use him after that.

L: Right.

C: It meant we had to hire someone new in the office, which was a pain because the money was bad and it was boring work. It was basically just stuffing envelopes, nothing even on the computers. But him quitting, it annoyed everyone in the office. But I stood up for him because I quite liked him. I defended him. Obviously we couldn't use him after that, but I didn't hold it against him.

Behind the arras, the bear sits back on his heels and tips his head towards the ceiling. He scratches his face. He looks pensive.

C: Anyway on his last day, which was a Friday, I think. I think it was a Friday. We were doing timesheets so it probably was. Anyway he was in the middle of the office, holding some envelopes, I think. Unless it's a bank holiday we tend to do them on a Friday. Everyone was around. I went up to him and so everyone could hear I told him that I understood his reasons for leaving, and I appreciated what he'd done, all stuff like that.

L: Right.

C: Right, so then I gave him a hug. You know, in the office with everyone around I gave him this really sort of warm hug. I think to be honest I kind of fancied him at the time. But I hugged him really tightly and usually, you know . . . you feel something. From him. But I didn't feel anything.

There are gasps and suggestive titters from the audience and Lisa and Carol pause to let the noise subside before continuing.

L: How long did it last?

C: Well, I pressed into him quite closely. But it wasn't even just that. I didn't feel anything from him. No warmth even. I got nothing back.

L: What did you do?

C: I just. Well, it finished, you know, and we got on with our work.

Unseen, the bear has silently left his spot behind the arras.

Clive's body rolls around, his hands wavering. Carefully he delineates to the bear each ache he suffers. His wife and daughter are in the kitchen, washing up. The little girl watches her uncle. Every twinge is given its own precise due. His feet swell inside his shoes, he gets these dull aches behind his right eyeball, he just sinks into armchairs and sofas these days and can't get up. He is a little drunk now and his monologue has taken on a maudlin cast. Pains are described and categorised. Hot and cold, internal and external, day and night. Every day, he says, something gets in his way. Cars start rolling away from the traffic lights before he's finished crossing, making him hurry up. There are building sites everywhere, he's often having to wait to cross while massive articulated lorries back into side streets in front of him. Cranes or vans block the pavement so he has to cross the road and then cross back to get around them, a waste of time. He picks up his glass and walks to the window. From the kitchen you can hear the sounds of an acoustic guitar playing and a man's voice singing. It is just the radio. Clive stands at the window, peering through the nets. He is afflicted, he is worn. Do you know, he says to the bear, not turning, what the purpose of the law is? Confused by the question, the bear says nothing. Can I have another drink, please? the girl asks. Clive, not turning, lifts up his left arm and waves his hand dismissively. He put his wine glass down on the sill. He puts both hands on the sill and leans heavily on it, looking out the nets. The purpose of the law, he says, is to take. You look at it, who does the law serve? It serves those that have and it serves them by allowing them to take from those who have less. That's the purpose of the law.

The little girl leads the bear into the bedroom by the hand. Do you like these? she says indifferently, pointing at something. She does not turn to see the bear's reaction. He looks at the things. Downstairs he can hear Louise and Clive bickering about something. He seems large in the room. She is looking in a drawer. Do you ever write a story? She turns to look at the bear, a pencil and paper in her hands. When my tutor comes over sometimes we write stories. She puts down the paper and picks up a doll. She looks at the doll then puts it down. The bear stands in the room and watches her do these things. Come and sit down, she goes, and we can write a story, OK? I start and then you write a sentence, OK? She holds the pencil uncomfortably in her fist. The bear watches her write. After a time she picks up the piece of paper, the squiggles on it too remote for the bear to make out, and goes and puts it in the drawer. She gets another piece of paper. You can start, she says. She hands him the pencil. The bear, pencil in paw, thinks for a moment. He writes. O, she goes, I remembered that the person's name should be Dennis, can you write it as Dennis? The bear nods. He writes.

It was a bright day. Dennis went up the hill.

He passes the piece of paper to the girl. She looks at it briefly and then looks up at the bear. She takes the pencil.

He came into the park he seen the body of a wooman.

The bear looks at what is written on the paper and then at the girl. The door behind opens and Louise comes in. You two are very quiet, she goes, what are you up to? She peers over the paper and her forehead crinkles in a way that the bear finds attractive. We're writing a story, says the girl, it's about Dennis. And who is Dennis? Louise asks, leaning in toward the girl. He's in the story, she answers. Write the next part! She's looking at the bear.

But the woman was OK, she got up and smiled at Dennis.

But then she had bled coming out of her.

So Dennis got her a plaster from his bag and gave it to her. "Thank you," she said, "you are a kind man."

No! said the girl, You're not doing it right!

She fell down again she was deaf at spiral park.

What is Spiral Park? asked Louise. The girl looked at her condescendingly. It's where we write stories about, she explained. The bear takes the piece of paper. For a moment he was just thinking about what would be in the story. From the way he holds the pencil loosely it could be observed that he seems to be tired with stories anyway, altogether. He glances at Louise; she is grinning at him. The girl looks impatient. He writes again.

So Dennis made sure the woman was OK but she was just sleeping. And she was OK. It was very beautiful at Spiral Park. He saw a lot of trees and also some grass.

OK, says the girl, reading. But that's not right again. She crosses the bit out. Do that bit again. The bear takes the piece of paper back again. What's wrong with it? asks Louise. I think that bit is nice. The bear writes.

Dennis tried to talk to her but she was deaf so she couldn't hear him.

No! Not deaf, she's not deaf, she's dead. I mean dead. Louise laughed. You don't spell dead like that, you've written that she is deaf. OK, replies the girl, but write it like I mean now. The bear crosses out the last bit.

Dennis was thinking about why she was dead. Why was she?

Louise gives the bear a hard look. He looks back at her. Regis, she says, don't put that. The girl takes the paper. The first side is now full of writing and crossings-out. She turns it over.

Dennis was on his skatebord and he went down a hill and fell over the wooman.

That's not how you spell woman, laughed Louise. Here, she takes the paper and writes the word Woman underneath. OK, says the girl. OK, but we need to do this next bit. Louise stands up. I'll be back in a minute, OK? She leaves the room.

Dennis had a good time at the park. It was easy for him and he made a lot of friends that day. He had fun on his skateboard.

But he fell down what is she ok he wanted to know.

"Are you OK?" he asked her.

But he picked up her and took her to her house and her mom screem.

He told the mum that it was OK, everything would be OK because the woman was only pretending, she was OK really.

But it got dark then and he can not find his way home.

Luckily he had a torch in his bag, which he used to find his house.

Louise comes into the doorway and says, We should get

going if dad is going to give us a lift. Are you done? The girl pulls a face and the bear hands her the pencil. He gets up. Louise leaves the room. The bear looks back for the paper but the girl is already standing up with it and putting it back into the drawer.

Something reminded the Recruitment Consultant of a joke; she told it to the girls in the office. A mouse goes to an elephant, Man, you're so big. The elephant goes back to the mouse, Man, you're so small. Yeah, goes the mouse, but I've been sick for six weeks.

The bear is at the cinema. He is seeing this film about an old White House chief of staff who had lost his fire getting it back after his protégé is turned into a dog by terrorists who have infiltrated the White House. The scene playing is the one where the old guy is running from several terrorists who have discovered his whereabouts. He is being reacquainted with gun use and has already, reluctantly, a little reluctantly, shot one of the terrorists. He's questioning whether he's doing the right thing, whether all this turmoil is worth the risk to save the White House and his country. Yeah, course it is. Yeah. He is gritting his teeth behind a pillar. The terrorists think they have lost him, but they are still cautious coming into the room. He turns, shoots one down and then dives behind a car for cover. The windows of the car smash in a hail of bullets. He sits with his back to the car, angling around, trying to look for an opening. There is a flashback to him standing at his train set watching the model trains go round an elaborate track. He has a big striped engine driver's hat on and he is saying Choo Choo! and fiddling with signals and lights and so on. One of the trains stops and he gives a little sigh and frowns. He picks it up and examines it then turns away and returns with a big oil can, which he holds in two hands, concentration on his face as he applies some oil to the wheels of the train. The camera pans from his face down to a close-up of him applying the oil. The picture fades back to him sitting by the car, and he is holding the gun in exactly the same way as he was holding the oil and the camera moves up to his face which, instead of a frown of mild concern, has become an angry grimace. He stands up suddenly, turns, and, with two flurries of fire, wastes the remaining pair of terrorists. He smiles through gritted teeth and wipes a bead of sweat from his brow. The bear is sitting in between his girlfriend, Helen, and her friend, Danielle. The bear has been going out with Helen for just over a month now and things are going OK.

One of the things that bothers the bear about his relationship with Helen is how undemonstrative she is, particularly in public. She gets embarrassed and shy about any displays of affection when anyone might be looking. The bear tries not to see this as a sign of her disapproval of him somehow, but it's difficult. Things are difficult with her too because she still lives with her parents and they are apparently very picky about who she goes out with, so the bear can't stay over at hers and her parents ask all kinds of difficult and embarrassing questions if she stays over at his or spends too much time with him. These things, which the bear sees as being irrelevant to how she decides to spend her time but which she sees as totally necessary if she wants to maintain a good relationship with the people she lives with, have already caused one or two arguments between them. The bear is happy, though, and mostly they get on. He isn't so keen on Danielle, who is sullen and uncommunicative towards him and often whispers and giggles things to Helen that he can't hear and assumes must be about him. Or, at least, they are secret from him, which is bad enough. In fact he deliberately skipped in front of Helen as they were walking down the cinema aisle so that he could sit in between them and stop them whispering to each other through the show.

The film winds towards its inevitable denouement. Nothing about the politics of the terrorists is made clear. No indication is made regarding where they obtain their money, which frustrates the bear. During a late scene in which the dog, suddenly sentient again, returns to save the old White House chief of staff from certain death at the hands of a particularly large, particularly swarthy terrorist, the bear takes his paws and pushes their heels into his eyeballs. Dramatic music, punctuated by dog barks, plays on the screen, which the bear now cannot see. What the bear sees is an accumulation of colour and light against black. The light has, but does not maintain consistently, a form. The bear can manipulate the shapes by applying and relieving the pressure of his paws against his eyes. Against a sparse field, the bear sees rapidly fluorescing jabs of orange light. The field turns red and is aggressive. The lights become murky and they converge at the centre of the bear's vision, forming one amorphous blob of indifferent hue. From out of the depths appears a white light of staggering intensity. It rises, engulfing the darkness, eating the darkness, diffusing a warmth that resonates through the bear's head and paws. A man on the screen shoots another man, but the bear does not see it. What he sees is a parade of white subsuming all darkness, all shade. It all goes white. White, the colour of death, the colour of harm. The bear leans back. No longer is he paying attention to the film, as though this white has eaten not just his vision but also his brain. This white, it has eaten everything, it has inflamed everything. In the cinema, Helen glances at Danielle and indicates the bear, who has fallen asleep. Danielle looks at him and rolls her eyes. On the screen, the dog has a terrorist by the throat and the former White House chief of staff is kicking the same terrorist in the head.

A man called Michael came into the recruitment agency. This guy Michael was looking for a job. The Recruitment Consultant called Carol was the one who interviewed him. Michael sat down in the office with the green carpets, on a chair with green upholstery. The Recruitment Consultant sat at a slight angle to him with some forms on a clipboard on her lap. – Hello Michael, she said.

– Hello, said Michael.

– And how are you doing today, you all right?

– I'm fine thanks. How are you?

– Shall we start, then? Now, you live, it says here, on Parkway Drive. Parkway Drive, now is that a cul-de-sac?

– It is, yeah. It's . . .

– All right, good. Now how do you think living in a cul-de-sac has affected the way you interact with both people and urban spaces?

– I'm sorry, what? Michael looked perplexedly at the Recruitment Consultant whose eyes were blue with indifference and antagonism.

– How do you think living in a cul-de-sac has affected the way you interact with both people and urban spaces?

– Well, I guess that, uh, it has made me appreciate that not all, uh, paths in life are open to us. I mean not just paths but I think that, uh . . . What I would say is that living in a cul-de-sac has shown me that the choices you make are in some ways less important than the choices you don't make.

– And this road you live on, it's in a suburb, isn't it? You don't live particularly central. What impact did this have on your childhood?

– My childhood? Michael seemed kind of confused at the question.

– Yes, your childhood. What kind of spaces do you encounter in the suburbs and how do they differ from the spaces you encounter in the city centre?

– Well, I, uh . . .

– What kind of school did you go to?

– I went to, uh, I went to just a normal secondary school.

– And you did well there, did you?

– I did OK, I think, yeah. The Recruitment Consultant paused and looked down at her clipboard which held a list of Michael's exam results on a piece of paper.

– You think you did OK. All right. She made a note of something. How do you get on with your mother, Michael?

– My mother?

– Yes, what kind of relationship do you have with your mother?

– Well, I . . . I suppose that I would characterise it as being generally positive. From interactions with my mother I have learned both the value of listening to your superiors but also of maintaining your own independence. I call to mind a time when she instructed me to tidy my room within a specific timescale. If I completed the task as requested then I would be rewarded with a trip to the park. This incentivised me to go into the task with a positive attitude and I did complete it. I was then able to go down the park with my bike.

– Do you ever have inappropriate thoughts about your mother, Michael?

– Yes, I have. I have in the past considered having intercourse with my mother. However what I've been able to do is take the scenarios I envisaged with my mother, the various approaches I would employ and the subsequent sexual encounters, and transpose them on to other, healthier, fantasy models such as women I have met or celebrities.

– And has that approach been successful?

– For the most part, but I feel that starting a temp job with you could only help me build on the skills I already have and also furnish me with new ones.

– Good, good. Now, Michael, do you drive?

– No, I don't drive.

– What do you think this says about you as a person?

– As a person I think this says about me that while I'm as goal orientated as the next man, I might use more unconventional methods of attaining that goal, such as for example getting the bus somewhere where the conventional wisdom would be to drive to that place. I also think that . . .

– . . . Sorry Michael, let me stop you there. Do you ever use pornography?

– Yes, I do.

– And what do you feel you've learned from it?

– I feel that I've learned the value of teamwork – that the more people on board on a task the more appealing the results can be. What I would say is not that too many cooks spoil the broth, but rather that many hands make light work.

– Do you think that the methodologies you've seen employed in pornography can translate into a business context?

– Absolutely, Carol, absolutely. Pornography has taught me a great deal about diversity and equality, both of which are incredibly important to me, and both of which I would want to build on in any job environment I was placed in. Another methodology which I think is translatable is a notion of group dynamics and hierarchies. In pornography there are clear hierarchies, but they are not so rigid as to be impermeable, those on the bottom can in some situations, if they perform well enough, rise to the top – I find this encouraging as someone who is looking to start a career. Most significantly, though, I feel that pornography demonstrates the lack of sincerity in business. When you look at a body in pornography you are rarely seeing a natural body. Similarly, when you go to work you don't display your real body, your real clothes, your real interests. When you look at pornography you are seeing the simulation of desire, not real desire. Similarly, when you go to work you simulate interest in the work you have to do. It's not enough for you to merely complete the tasks you're allocated, you have to give the appearance of being interested and invested in the completion of those tasks. I firmly believe that if you ape the facial expressions, the mannerisms, the mastery of your own desires and responses displayed in pornography then you are on the right track to becoming a great employee.

– OK, Michael. Where do you see yourself being in five years' time?

– In five years' time I see myself in a demanding, high-level admin role, such as being the administrator for a powerful member of a large organisation.

– And what skills do you think you need before you are able to take on such a role as the role you have just described to me?

– I think that negotiating the humiliating and unfulfilling world of temp work will equip me with the skills necessary to work as an administrator for a powerful man. I will learn that other people's poor planning is my crisis, I will learn that I am expendable. I will learn that a company is prepared to spend far more on one lunch for a few visitors than on a salary for me for a week's work. I will learn that if I slip up, if I am seen to contravene some regulation, if I upset somebody, whether it is my fault or not, I can be got rid of. I can be cast aside. I'll learn that. I'll learn that it's better to say nothing than to complain, to criticise, to offer ideas for improvement. I'll learn that the best way is to keep quiet and sit in front of my computer, whether I have work to do or not, and not bother anyone.

– Good, OK, good. Right, good. Now. Is there anything you want to ask me?

– Yes, in fact there is. I would like to ask you. What type of animal, out of any type of animal that you could choose, would you choose to be and why?

– Good question. Interesting question. Well, Michael, I have to say, if I could choose any animal out of any animal and I would be that animal, the animal I would probably choose would be a bear.

– And why would you choose a bear?

– I would choose a bear because a bear is both a metaphor for strength and an embodiment of real physical strength. A bear is both unyielding to the dangers of nature and inexorably tethered to that nature. Bears are both an enemy of man and a demonstration by god of what man could become if man was greater, more benevolent, less conceited, less arrogant, more dynamic, less divisive. The bear hints at what man could have been. The bear's silence is more profound than any human speech. The bear's grace is deeper than that of any saint. The bear's indifference is more profound than any human politics. I would be a bear.

It took the Recruitment Consultant a long time to realise she was going deaf. It began in her left ear. Or, at least, this is where she noticed it beginning. At first, her deafness was merely theoretical. What she seemed to feel was an accumulation of wax in her left ear. In the office she would make jokes about it. Ha ha ha. Everyone would laugh benignly at her Whatting and Pardoning, her mock calls for a hearing aid or even an ear trumpet! Ha ha. Ha ha ha. Seriously though. Seriously. It isn't that funny. It kind of hurts, she would say. And then someone would say, Have you tried putting olive oil in them? And she would reply, What? and look around mock-mystified, like she hadn't heard what they were saying. That's the kind of laid-back situation there was in that office. It was that kind of situation. Her doctor saw no infection, merely an accumulation of wax. She was told to put olive oil in them twice a day, which she did, for two weeks, which she did. Near the end of the two-week period she noticed that her hearing in her left ear had significantly decreased. Lying in bed one evening she listened to the noise of the traffic on the main road outside her bedroom window. Her left ear was on the pillow, all the hearing she was doing was with her right ear. She switched sides so that her right ear was on the pillow. She noticed that she could no longer hear the traffic.

In surreptitious moments, she would push her little finger

right into the left ear and oscillate it and waggle it. She would scrape at the wax on the walls of the ear-canal. Her finger would come away sticky, often with a small, dense, pile of dark wax on the tip. She would, at times, taste the wax: its sourness, its bitter flavour. She would hold her nose, keep her mouth tightly shut, close the lobe of her right ear with a finger and blow out hard for several seconds. The effect of this was painful and disorientating, and it only seemed to make her hearing worse, but she continued to do it. After blowing, there would be a few seconds of calm, then there would be long streams of popping noises in her ear, alternating with high screeching noises. This, she felt, was the sound of the wax clearing, of pressure blasting through the blockage. But it was not. After doing it for prolonged periods her ear would ache profoundly and her hearing in that ear would reduce. At other times she would hold the lobe down and squeeze it tightly. There would be a feeling of pressure, at times a feeling of release. If she held it down for long enough, there would be a similar popping and screeching effect. Sometimes, on releasing the lobe there would be a feeling – an optimistic feeling – that her hearing had improved, but it never lasted very long. For the Recruitment Consultant, hearing loss in one ear was a disorientating process. She began to hear cars approaching on her left side in her right ear first. In time she learned to distinguish between sounds actually coming from her right side and those merely appearing to because of her hearing deficiency. She craved yawning. Yawning seemed to hold some kind of key to unblocking her ears. As she yawned she would try to force the yawn outwards, towards her ear canals, trying to find the key organisation of movements that would force the pressure of the yawn in the right direction and unblock the ears. But it never came.

At the clinic, the nurse confirmed that the wax in the Recruitment Consultant's ears was soft enough and, with a machine, irrigated them. The Recruitment Consultant held a metal canister next to her ear and felt the warm wax and water drip into it. The nurse commented on how much wax there was. There was a lot of wax. The Recruitment Consultant did not look into the canister after the irrigation was complete. Her ears still felt blocked, but the nurse assured her that it was just water in them now, and that would clear in the next couple of days. She thanked the nurse and left the clinic. It was a bright day and she had taken leave from work. The sun was shining. She was on the high street. In her right ear, noises sounded loud and crisp. It was great. Her left ear still felt blocked and heavy. In it there was some kind of ambient echo of the clearer noises coming from the right. She was walking towards the bus stop. The sun went behind a cloud and it felt suddenly cold. The bus drove past her towards the stop. She began to run. As she accelerated, she could feel the water sloshing in her left ear. She ran. She felt a warm trickle on her left cheek. Water ran from her ear down her cheek and into her collar. With clarity and volume she heard the noise of the bus stopping. She slowed her run as she reached the back of the queue for the bus. She was elated. Her left ear heard what her right did. No longer a dull approximation of the sounds around her. No longer a muted, imbalanced portrayal, but real clear noise. She stood up straight. The sun returned. She felt like leaving the bus queue, going back to the high street and buying music, something she could listen to. She felt like blowing money. She whistled a couple of bars of Celine Dion's 'The Heart Will Go On'. She liked hearing the effect. It was great. She got on the bus and paid the money. The noise of the engine idling was pleasing to her. Its mordant thud, its jitter, it promised so much. The sounds of the change in the plastic tray, the driver's hands sorting through it, handing it back, it promised so much. The tenor, the cadence of people's voices, the squeak of mobile phones, all these ambient sounds were full of promise to her. She looked out of the window down a high street on which the sun was shining. It was full of people and shops and sun.

The bus moved off. It pulled away from the kerb. The engine rushed and roared. It surged, it pulsed. It was the sound-track to a dream of motion. Her recovery was soundtracked by a bus engine and two old women chatting about a dog. Apparently he, the dog, would eat anything, living or dead. It was disgusting some of the things you saw him eat. And that was just what you saw, you know. And his appetite! He was forever stealing from the cat's bowl. The cat didn't get a look-in these days. You had to lock the dog outside to feed the cat in the kitchen. And then the cat's up on all the worktops, making a mess! It was certainly a chore, keeping that dog.

At the junction, it was difficult to tell who pulled away too

quickly, whether it was the bus or the other guy. The other
guy's car swerved and he hit the passenger side of another
car. The passenger side was fortunately empty. He was
all right. And the driver of the car he crashed into, he was
angry, but he was all right. He, they both, heard what happened to the bus before he turned and saw it. He turned
and saw that the bus had gone into a wall. The wall was
the wall of a newsagents. He walked towards the wreckage. This other guy was running on adrenalin now. There
was a lot of dust in the air. Everything was covered with it.
The newsagent was nowhere to be seen. The bus had gone
right into the drinks cabinet and cans and bottles of sticky
liquid were fizzing everywhere. There were a lot of people
around shouting, but like in a film, this other guy couldn't
hear them. It seemed kind of silent. People were coming
out of houses and cars all along the street to converge on
this scene. Soon an ambulance would arrive. They would
find that the bus driver, the Recruitment Consultant and
the two old women were dead. Who would be feeding that
dog now? The rest of the people on the bus were OK, or
hurt but OK. They all turned out to be OK. The newsagent
had just gone into the back for something when the crash
happened, so he was OK too. He had. For now, though,
this other guy stood at the mouth of the wreckage. Some
people, perhaps they were from the bus, stumbled around
him. He barely saw them. There was Doctor Pepper on
the bottom of his trousers and his shoes and the dust was
sticking to the Doctor Pepper. He expressed annoyance at
the dust on his trousers. No one else really heard it, the
road was so cluttered with other noises. This other guy, he

was in a bit of a world of his own. He turned around to see the man whose car he'd smashed into waving a bit of paper, he could hear him shouting the word 'insurance'. He did not faint. He did not fall.

Though he wasn't aware of it at the time, the question that faced the bear when he made the transition into humanity was whether he wanted to trade a short and happy life for a long and miserable one. A short and happy life. One of the things he was able to notice after he joined people, joined humanity, was that his perception of time had changed. He seemed to age more slowly. His claws and his fur grew less quickly. What he deduced from this was that he could be whoever he said he wanted to be. However he perceived himself, that's what he became, and nature, whatever that was, would fall into step. He lost some of his bulk, his arms seemed to shorten a little and his legs lengthen. When his claws grew back they grew back flatter and less thick. What he failed to deduce from this was that though an animal may choose to be human, what is human is not immutable. Humanity expands to fit. Its boundaries sprawl and eat. The bear did not sneak over the border, rather the border flooded over and enveloped him. By entering humanity you agree to pay, you agree to owe, and the only conditions required to enter are to pay and to owe. And humanity greedily accepts anyone who wants to be part of it, for the more people that owe, the more is owed in total and the richer those few who are owed become. Similarly, once you are in, humanity grips tightly and will not let go. It's not possible to change your mind and simply opt out. The bear found that his fur grew thinner and sparser, patches of his skin became blank, pink and hairless. Over time he felt his musculature waning. He became more conscious of the weather. The cold would pucker his bare skin and bring it out in goosebumps and the sun would burn his flesh a dark pink. He felt changes in temperature more keenly, and regularly struggled to find appropriate clothing to suit him for a whole day. Often he would venture out in the mornings with a coat on over a jumper and shirt and be sweating and uncomfortable before he reached work. Or he would leave the house in just a shirt and be wet and cold, envious of everyone else with their coat on and their hood up. He felt and felt keenly the burden of his owing.

The bear is stood in the corner of their room. He looms over it, he is hunched underneath the ceiling. He and his girlfriend are arguing. This would be where the relationship ends. You don't have any ambition, she says to him. She is stood in front of him, head down, hands on her hips. She looks up, her eyes are damp. The bear is still there in the corner. He winces.

The bear is at this job where there is nothing to do what-
soever. It's in an office right in the city centre, near to the
town hall. The people there, he gets on OK with them. They
sit around and chat with each other and try to pass the time
until they can go home. What they like to do most, though,
is diss each other. Their favourite game is just sitting there
dissing. They kill time by dissing each other. The bear is
good at this game. There would come a point in the day
where someone dissed the bear. A point when someone
dissed him raw. He would get up, amble over to that person,
stand looming there above them, looking down from his
black eyes, steady his massive bulk and, in his surpris-
ingly nasal, high voice, declaim: I kicked you. I kicked your
dog. I kicked your house. I kicked your mug. I kicked your
dinner. I kicked your dog into your dinner. Your dog died
when I kicked it. I kicked your mother. I kicked your horse.
I kicked your stereo. Your mom fell down when I kicked
her. Your horse went lame when I kicked it. I gave your car
a flat tyre because I kicked it. I kicked your grandmother.
I kicked your boyfriend. I kicked your family bush. Your
boyfriend died when I kicked him. At the funeral I kicked
his coffin. I kicked your telephone. I kicked your chin. I
kicked your head. I kicked your shoes. I kicked your back.
I kicked your ears. I kicked your pizza. I kicked your kettle.
I kicked your tissue. I kicked your window. I kicked your
car. Your grandmother went deaf because I kicked her in

the ears. The glass from your window went into your pizza when I kicked it. I kicked your vegetable garden. I kicked your drug habit. I kicked your hamster over a wall. I kicked your wall. I kicked your mirror. The glass from your mirror fell into your dog when I kicked it. I kicked your head in. I kicked your table. I kicked your dad's boyfriend. When I kicked your table your dinner went onto your mother . . . This bear, if he had to, if the diss merited it, could go on all night.

One afternoon at this particular job, there is some fuss. Someone from top management is coming in to have a look around the office. Despite the fact that these people always work far less hard and earn far more money than the average employee of any company, they are given deference and respect wherever they go. Who knows why? It's a mystery. These bastards would snap your pension right out from under you and spend it on golf club membership given half a chance, yet when you meet them you have to shake their hand and hear them be condescending towards you and laugh at their terrible jokes and pretend not to be aware of their ignorance.

The top management man comes in. His face is white and gaunt. His teeth are all yellow. He shuffles in. Everyone stands. He ambles around the office. He puts his hand on the shoulders of the women working there and they drink in the odour of his sweat. And it is them that pay for him to stand and sweat. Their work pays for his shirt to be dry-cleaned, the sweat they caused will be washed right out of the shirt, paid for by their work. The man does not acknowledge this but stands there, in the office, as though he had some right, because of the size of his salary, to stand there.

He goes around talking to some of the people working there. He asks them patronising questions and seems amused by their replies. He is in a position where he can say whatever he wants, he is the most senior person in the room; everyone else has to make sure what they say suits him.

He comes to the bear. He stands and looks at the bear for a moment. His look changes. He takes a step or two backwards. He turns to the man next to him, who is the manager of that particular branch office. He turns to this man and he says very loudly, This is not a man. This is a bear.

The bear faces the guy. Suddenly it is very loud in the office. All the other employees, the guys he thought were his mates, come charging at him. They hit at him with their fists, they pull at his clothes, they drive him from the building.

The bear leaves the office. He is in the city centre. He comes out into a square. It is a big open square. The first thing he sees is a dog traversing the square, followed by a man in a grubby brown jacket. The dog is brown too. The bear stands there looking at the dog and where the dog is going. The dog is going across the square. The dog is traversing the square. The bear, too, begins to traverse the square, but in a different, in a perpendicular direction. The square contains a variety of architectural styles. Being the thoughtful type, as he traverses, the bear contemplates these styles. He turns and looks at the building he has just left. It is a squat office building. The windows are mirrored on the outside. It has a glass door. Above the door is the name of the building in gold plastic letters on a black plastic background. The effect of the building on the eye is something like the effect of a deflated bouncy castle on a party of young children. The bear traverses. The town hall is a building with Greek ionic columns surrounding the entrance, gothic stone gargoyles, a phallic blue glass postmodern extension jutting out of the side at an angle of around thirty degrees (reputedly the leader of the council's office is in the very tip of this phallus, a room which gets progressively narrower and lower the further in you go. Reputedly the very smallest part of this room, so far at the back that one has to lean in on the tip of one's toes and stretch out the tip of one's middle finger, has a button which, in times of trouble, would, if pressed, detach the leader of the council's office from the rest of the extension and fire it in the direction of America), a medieval tapestry design depicted in mosaic over the front porch, a maroon banner running down the entire side of the building proclaims in yellow letters YOU AND I ARE ALL OUR ART and has a child's drawing in crayon of either a pig or a pig-faced man laughing out at you. The town hall is also in this square. Beside the town hall, practically penetrated by the postmodern extension is a skyscraper made of silver metal and glass. It is several stories higher than anything in the vicinity and its position ensures that the wind always blows hard across the square which the bear traverses, buffeted by that wind, the dog's fur tussled by that wind, the man's grubby brown coat pressed against himself by that wind. The square contains seven trees and the leaves are rustled by that wind. The square contains a fountain depicting Zeus as a swan, raping Leda. The swan's oversized phallus emits a jet of water towards Leda's oversized vagina which is supposed to receive it but the wind caused by the skyscraper pushes the water away so that it merely splashes over her thighs and stomach.

There are benches in the square which nobody sits on.

There are four exits from the square. One leads you through the narrow passage between the town hall and the skyscraper. The bear can see a lot of men in suits struggling against the wind or being pushed along by it walking down that passage in either direction. This passage leads towards the ring road and the hotels and office blocks that surround the city centre. Another exit leads you towards shops and the bear takes this exit. The wind drops.

The bear walks down a street lined with shops. It is hard going, to keep up with all the people going this way and that. It is hard for the bear to find a pair of trousers that he can fit into or shoes that he can wear and yet he sees in shop windows trousers and shoes and covets them. A pair of brown shoes, he covets. A plastic mannequin wearing a pair of fetching grey trousers, he covets those trousers. The city centre is full of people and they all covet. What they want versus what they can have, we might conjecture that the city centre's existence is founded upon this fissure. For this bear it is a fissure all the more profound as he stands head and shoulders above most of the others on the street, as his girth is vaster than most of the others on the street, his nose colder, his claws sharper. And yet in the big pockets of his slacks he has money and he could hunch up his shoulders and squeeze through the door of a shop and pick up a pair of trousers and put them down on the counter and pay for them like it was nothing at all. The bear can stand astride the fissure for a second, just like anyone can, just like there was nothing to it. Of course, though, he and everyone knows that that, nah, it's more than nothing.

The road is full of men, women and kids. Full of them. The bear walks down it and looks at them. The bear looks at the men and knows that if it came to it he could probably take them. He could probably beat them up. They walk around in their coats. Their hair is grey, their eyes are slack. The bear sees them with their friends, their families, carrying bags, pushing their kids along the street. The bear walks and sees them all. Their noise – the collective sounds of laughter, scratching, wheels, arguments, sniffing, gesticulating, exclaiming, coughs, digestion, hair, children noises, croaking, chewing, stops, clicks, claps, clacks, gurgling, becomes a single cacophony that bounces off the high shopfronts and all around the narrow street. Cars going by also make intermittent noise. The bear cannot fail to hear these sounds and be moved by them. This street has an awesome density of visual and sonic detail. The bear moves through the fug of noise, its texture changing with each minuscule inclining of his head. The principal direction of the street is south-east. The bear considers as he walks, for a time, the etymology of the word 'tool' as a pejorative. Some kid the bear sees wearing a leather jacket and with a haircut. Is he a tool? The bear feels he would have to know the guy better to be able to say that. Perhaps he is decent as a guy. Perhaps he is a tool, but still also decent. Is that possible?

The bear continues to walk through the city centre. All the places that are Pizza Hut, all the places you can get a sandwich in, all the shops selling cards or selling cloth animals, the things that used to be other things, the road-works, the luxury flats, the carparks, billboards, canals. Et cetera et cetera. This bear, he walks. And then, just like that, he stops. Why? The bear stops because as he walks past a particular shop window, the shop happened to be a Caffè Nero, at a table in the window of Caffè Nero, at a table in the window of Caffè Nero which has a cup of coffee on it and a piece of cake, at this table in the window of Caffè Nero which has a cup of coffee and a piece of cake on it a man, sitting, catches the bear's eyes and will not stop staring, at this table, a table in the window of Caffè Nero, a man, corpulent, red-skinned, with a flat stub of a nose, big broad hands, small unhappy eyes, this man sits at the table with his coffee and his piece of cake in the window of Caffè Nero and looks out hard at our bear who stops and looks back at him. Slowly, the man, his eyes fixed on the bear's and the bear's fixed on his, he puts his big hands on the table, he almost tips over his coffee, he almost flattens his cake, he, hands on the table, pushes his bulk up out of his chair so that he is standing. He stands and looks at the bear. The man's face is set. The two stare directly at each other through the glass of the Caffè Nero window. The man is wearing a big cream-coloured suit. His body bulges out of it. His hands, still palm down on the table, are raw nauseous pink with flat grey blocks of nails. They stand staring at each other for a long time, though less time than it might take to read a paragraph of description about them staring at each other. Caffè Nero steams up. Caffè Nero goes fuzzy. The cars and sounds around the bear fracture, lose their solidity, become intangible, theoretical. These merely theoretical sounds do not register with the bear. It is hard to say whether they are loud enough to penetrate the glass and register with the man who still stands, staring. On the table in the window of Caffè Nero, though, the man seems still, the coffee in the cup has begun, almost imperceptibly, to vibrate. The man's hands seem aggressively pinker. His face likewise. Recognition spills over the bear like a horse over a jump. The bear's paws begin to shake. The bear sweats. The man behind the window holds a hand out to the bear, holds it palm up, his eyes implore. The bear turns, the bear begins to jog, then run. He runs from the city centre. The thing is, the thing the bear realised, is that behind the glass it was not a man at all. It was not a man. It was another bear.

The bear does not stop running until he is outside the city centre. There is no clear demarcation of this transition, only a feeling. Nonetheless it is a profound feeling. The bear looks back and sees the big buildings of the city centre. Principal among them are the giant glass office block that made the square so windy and also, closer to him, a big beige indoor shopping complex. The view of the complex is obscured by a low railway bridge. The direction that the bear has run in has taken him to a part of town full of derelict warehouses, old factories and dark brick buildings. Ahead of him, now that he turns away from the city centre, he can see clusters of tower blocks not far away. He walks slowly for a moment, catching his breath. To his left there is a patch of concrete ground protected by a green plastic wire fence. Scruffy plants grow up out of the splits in the concrete and beyond the fence there is a brick building with dusty windows, smashed glass, rotted doorframes, exposed patches of tileless roof, a sign with missing letters and the paint of the sign worn away to scars of blank wood, crisp packets and old cans of drink piled up against the wall among other unidentifiable detritus, a gutter leaking a filthy yellow liquid in a thin stream down the wall around which a grey moss grows, a pushed-over chimney stack, the scutter of mice, a hint of insects, a dog's bark, a cry of collapse, a wind that shrieks out the windows, a glass rattle. Inside there is the dust from fingernails, hair and skin, dust on the old machinery, sperm dried up on the floor, tears dried into the woodwork, blood dried in spray up the wall and gone brown, shit gone hard in pellets in the corner, dark patches of piss, green droplets of phlegm, little spots of saliva, nails bitten off and spat out and gone brittle on the floor, eyelashes pulled out with fingernails, clumps of dog hair and cat hair and rat hair, dead insect legs and wings now desiccated, the machinery and the door hinges and the window hinges and clasps gone rusty, the electricity is dead, the glass in the lightbulbs is smashed, the dogs that lived there all died, the rats ate out their corpses, eyes first, the rats died and were eaten by insects, the insects died and their bodies were blown out to the countryside and planted and became flowers, the blades of the machines are blunt, the buttons don't do anything any more, they don't switch anything on, they don't push or pull anything, they don't raise or lower anything, nothing moves except what gets moved by the wind and the machines don't get moved by the wind, the wind moves the spider's webs, the wind moves the dust, the wind moves the hair, it piles up in the corners, it is from a variety of animals, it contains insects, it contains dust, the dust is an agglomeration of the blood, the sperm, the phlegm, the sweat, the piss, the shit, the fingernails, the skin, the tears of the men and animals that were there and it contains the memories, joyful and sorrowful, of all those men and all those animals and they reverberate around the place, the memories themselves become an agglomeration, they fight with each other, they join together, they form alliances and enemies but there is a space outside their politics where they band together to try to protect the building from the decay caused by water and wind but ultimately they know they cannot win, they can only delay the process infinitesimally, the wind and rain are indifferent, the building will not stand, it will fall, it will go.

The bear looks through the fence, past the concrete patch, through the window, past the machinery right to the back corner where the dust and hair is piled up, right into the pile, closer in so that the fine grains of dust are visible as separate, singular entities, into one of the grains, its mottled surface, further in so that the dust particle appears to be the craggy surface of a grey, alien planet with vast plains and valleys and deeper, down into the valley, the surface breaking up into packs of molecules clustered together humming and swarming, down into one atom of one molecule, through shells of zipping electrons, through the nuclear envelope, down further, deeper than the tiniest quark, so minute that everything is enveloped in cavern-ous, devastating white, a white that covets, a white that mourns, a white that slowly fades and turns blue-grey closer in, turns a grey-blue that seems to have some amor-phous darker grey on the horizon, a blue-grey that gives way to this darker grey, the grey begins to take shape and form, coalesce into different blobs of colour which become increasingly distinct, taking on texture and shade, clearly this is the shape of a universe, then a galaxy, a solar system, a star, a blue and green planet, a nation, a city, a street, a bear looking at a green wire fence, past a concrete patch, through the window of a derelict building, past the machin-

ery, into the corner where dust and hair is piled up, right
into the pile . . .

The bear walks past any number of buildings like this.
There is almost no one around, and no traffic. People used
to work here, but now, these days, mostly they don't. The
bear walks past another fenced-off patch of ground that is
filled with empty parked lorry trailers protected by coils
of barbed wire. A sign says how expensive it is to put your
lorry trailer here. In a yellow kiosk a man watches a plastic
monitor that shows the lorries filmed from the upper
corner of an adjacent building, from above, filmed from
behind showing their empty interiors, filmed from the side
showing the logos on the sides of the trailers advertising a
lot of things in big letters. The bear turns at the corner, now
he is heading west, the afternoon sun glares, a train goes
across the bridge and the sun glares on it. At the far corner
there is a pub and, next to it, a former school building that
has been turned into an office furniture warehouse.

Far in front of the bear is a woman pushing a pushchair
towards the sun. The road curves down towards the dual
carriageway. She walks very slowly, this woman. The pushchair is laden with shopping bags full of frozen food. The
bear, getting closer, can see that it is all frozen food. To
his right hulk the tower blocks. The dual carriageway is up
ahead. Stubs of plants spring up at the corners of buildings. The woman is very large and her hair is greasy. The
bear cannot see the kid in the buggy. She is a despairing
woman with a mouth. That he is able to see. She goes down

the hill, this woman. Before the bear reaches her she turns off and crosses the road. She turns into a narrow alley bordered by two tower blocks. The alley is walled on both sides by grey concrete. Each wall has some graffiti. The graffiti says derisive things in illegible script. It says such things as a particular woman is a slag, or a particular other woman is a bitch or a particular footballer is a dickhead or a particular woman is a cunt. The bear stops and watches this woman negotiate this alley. The tower blocks above and the walls of the alley force the wind through it at alarming force. The woman hunches her shoulders and leans low over the handles of the buggy as she enters. The kid in there, what must it think? As she enters the alley, the woman's scrunchie is blown out of her hair and the pink donut of fabric is flung in an upward gust away in the direction of one of the blocks of flats. Her lank hair streams out almost vertically above her head and her shopping bags are flung back. She braces herself against it, she is forced back half a step and then, with renewed strength, soldiers on, shoulder braced against one of the walls. The force of the wind drives the thin fabric of her trousers against her legs and balloons it out behind her. She moves forward by pushing off the wall with her shoulder and driving the buggy towards the opposite wall, bracing herself for a moment there before pushing off again, occasionally being thrown back, sometimes fighting through. Just as she is resting a moment a tiny yapping dog enters the alley and is whipped up and thrown towards the woman, blurted out by the wind it scrapes along her face and then is sent scrambling onto the pavement. Continually, crisp packets and bits of newspaper and plastic bags and other detritus are blown into the alley and out of the alley. At a certain point the alley curves slightly to the right and widens. At this point the wind is strongest. The woman turns there slightly into the wind and is forced back. The kid's arms are visibly flung back and its hands claw and scrape at the invisible wind in vain.

A piece of magazine blows against the bear's leg where he is standing watching the woman and sticks there. There is an inset quotation on it in bold yellow writing saying, 'I just play tennis and do good cocaine and record albums. It's pretty sweet.' And there is a picture of a man with a jacket, scarf and hairstyle.

The bear stands and watches and the woman tries again and again to force her way through the turn in the alley. He looks up at the tower blocks. He looks down towards the dual carriageway. An old man enters the alley and, flattening himself against the wall, he goes crablike along it towards the woman. He is strong, this old man. His brown jacket splays out as he turns slightly towards her. Their mouths move, his first, then the woman's. The woman turns towards him and her hair blows into her face. He puts his hand on the handle of the buggy and tries to push it forward. The woman punches him. As he momentarily reels from the punch the wind picks up, thrusting the buggy and the woman against the wall and pitching the man into the air for a second and then down heavily onto the ground, where he lies, motionless except for what motion is caused by the wind. There is some respite, some let-up, and the woman pushes through the turn and is no longer visible.

The bear reaches that dual carriageway.

A dual carriageway is a wide road divided by a fenced central reservation. The route the bear has taken enters the dual carriageway at its most congested point. Just ahead, a roundabout funnels in cars from six other roads. On the bear's side there is a line of car showrooms. Nearest to him is an empty one. A poster in the window tells you the nearest other place to get that type of car now that this showroom is closed. The glass frontage of the showroom is thick with dust. There are no cars in the showroom. The floor of the showroom is strewn with junk, bits of wood and pieces of plastic. In the centre of the showroom there is a plastic stand for brochures, sitting empty. The fore-court stands empty, a desk inside is empty. It is all there, empty. Beside the showroom are a couple of big plastic recycling bins, overflowing with shards of coloured glass. On the other side of the dual carriageway, behind all the cars, is a dismal row of shops. A sex shop with a thick metal grille behind which are three mannequins dressed in black leather. The mannequins are set up in sexy poses and the outfits they wear are revealing. But they are mere plastic. If the bear could cross the road he could go into that shop, but there is no crossing. The next shop is selling some mobile phones. They've got the mobile phones there, in the window. A whole range of mobile phones. See in the window there, of that shop, next to the sex shop. Between the sex shop and the newsagents. Mobile phones. They've got mobile phones in the window, they've got more mobile phones inside the shop there. They've got, in the window there, they've got the mobile phones. The mobiles, you can call them mobiles. They've got the mobiles there in the window, the mobile phones, they've got the mobiles: it's a mobiles shop. It's a mobile phone shop. They sell mobiles, they sell chargers, they sell sim cards, they sell spare batteries. A lot of things, they sell. In the mobile phone shop. They sell mobile phones. You can see them there, the window: mobile phones, the mobiles. It's not ... they don't sell fruit in there, just the mobile phones and mobile phone accessories. Just that. But that's still a lot. Mobile phones. Mobile phones, mobiles and mobile phone accessories such as a sim card or a mobile phone phone charger. They don't sell fruit or fish and chips. None of that. Not fish, not chips. In the window there, some mobile phones. They have mobiles in the shop and to advertise them, to draw people in off the street who might want a mobile they put some of them, the best ones, the nicest ones, in the window. You pay them some money and they give you a mobile phone and you can use it to call up the shop and thank them for giving you a mobile phone. Then they might ring you up to thank you for buying a mobile phone, a mobile they would probably call it, in their expert vernacular, they might ring you up to thank you for buying a mobile from them, for giving them some money in exchange for a mobile phone, a mobile. When they ring you your mobile phone will ring and you can have any ringtone you want on your mobile phone. On your mobile. In the window of that shop they have some of the mobile phones. You can get one and have any ringtone you want on it. Busted I'm Glad I Crashed The Wedding is one you could have, one ringtone. You don't have to have the whole song, just your favourite part as the ringtone. The ringtone on your mobile phone. On your mobile. You would probably call it a mobile these days. A mobile with a ringtone. You could have the part of Busted I'm Glad I Crashed The Wedding where they sing I'm Glad I Crashed The Wedding looped so that you hear it multiple times before you pick up your mobile phone. So when the shop rings you to thank you for buying a mobile phone – a mobile they would probably call it, they are experts, they would probably call it a mobile, just a mobile, they wouldn't bother saying mobile phone, they probably would have to say mobile phone lots of times every day so shortening it to mobile means they can say it twice as often but in the same amount of time – then Busted I'm Glad I Crashed The Wedding would play – not the whole song, not the whole of it, just the bit you wanted, just the bit where they sing I'm Glad I Crashed The Wedding and maybe a bit with a guitar put into a loop that goes on over and over again until you pick the phone up. Hii! Hello! No, thank you! Thank you for selling me this mobile phone! Oh yes, oh right, OK, I will call it a mobile from now on. That will save a lot of time! Bye! Thanks! Byee! See you! Bye! Bye! See you later! See you! You might say that to them when they call. In the window of this shop there are mobile phones, mobiles. You say mobiles these days. It's quicker. It saves you time. You can see black mobiles, silver ones, even pink ones. Some of them have colour screens. Some of them have cameras.

You can play games on them. Mobiles, the mobile phones. There is a shop over the road from the bear selling mobile phones, selling mobiles, they have some in the window and a neon sign that says 'Mobiles'. The door of the shop is glass and you can see through it, you can see that there are more mobiles there, in the shop. Not just in the window. It's not a shop with mobile phones, mobiles, in the window and then selling something else like fruit or fish and chips or staplers inside. It's a mobiles shop that sells mobiles and has mobiles in the window. The mobiles, the mobile phones. You sometimes see them called mobiles. It doesn't mean mobile like a baby would have. Like a thing that hangs down over a crib and has, say, a duck, a horse and a pig on it hanging down over the crib for the baby to look at and play with. Mobiles doesn't mean that. It means mobile phones. Mobiles that a baby would have are different to mobiles that an adult would have. An adult might make a mobile for a baby out of coathangers and a small toy duck but you can't make a call on that kind of mobile. Mobiles they have, mobiles. Mobiles that you can make a call on, lots of different ones they have. That's what they have in that shop window. Mobile phones, mobiles.

Next to the mobile phone shop is a newsagent.

Next to the newsagent is a small bank branch. It is a branch of a big 'high street' bank. The guys that work in there are squeezed into pens to protect the money they have. They sit like pigs behind glass screens. Money isn't everything but money is a thing. The bear happens to have an account with this bank. Just happens to. The bear, Regis the bear, ruminates on his interactions with this particular bank during the time he's had an account with them. He considers his position in relation to this particular bank, which could really be any bank as they are all pretty much the same. They are all pretty much the same in that they are all pretty much just a bunch of robbing bastards, this bear thinks. The times when they have plainly robbed a few quid out of his account! The money that he worked for! Hours' worth of his time, just gone to them, gone to nothing. It is not a pleasant rumination, this one. No pleasure is to be gained from an experience with a bank. The sun is getting lower in the sky. The sun will go down today like it always does. It is the afternoon and no pleasure is ever gained from interaction with a bank. A child could kick a ball, a child used to be able to just kick a ball, now what do we have? Because of these guys it can't. It can't kick a ball. A vegetable used to taste like a vegetable, now what does it taste like? You used to be able to leave your door open at night. Now look at it. Now look at how life is. Because of these guys. Because of these businessmen, these bankers. Now look at how the times are. A man used to be able to take his hands and put rings on them and walk around with his hands in his pockets. Now what do you have? His hands are in the vice. The rings have been melted down into metal blocks which are kept in dark vaults. The man's fingers have been snipped off and stored in vaults in case a banker might ever need some spare fingers. A woman used to be free to take a dog for a walk by the canal on a sunny day. Now what do you have? The dog is put to work in the fields, the canal is full of dead children, the woman is stuck at her computer, the sun has been pulled down and used to light private beaches and gardens of the rich. You used to be able to have an account with a few quid in it. Just a few quid! Now these robdogs – these bloody robdogs! – take that few quid from you at the drop of a hat. A bird used to fly nowhere, a bird didn't have to know where it was going. But what direction can a bird take now that it is chained to a plough and trapped in an indoor field? These guys, these guys have done this to a bird. A man used to be able to ride a horse through the wilderness. Now what do you have? The man can't find parking for his car even though the wilderness is now all car parks, the horse has been melted down to make envelope glue for the bankers to send memos in envelopes all about how much money they are robbing off you each day. A man could carry his boombox out onto the street and listen to some sounds. Now the streets are full of billboards advertising banks, the boombox is full of news reports about money and the man's hands have been filled with debt so full that he can no longer grip. This is what these guys have done to us. All for a few quid! It used to be that a man could remember the good times and the bad times of his life in peace, it used to be that a woman could fondly look back on her life, the mistakes and the triumphs. It used to be that! But what do we have now? What the hell is going on now? A man in a suit comes and sucks your memories out of you with a vacuum nozzle and you have to pay him a few quid to look at them on a little scratched mobile phone screen. This man, this guy in a suit, tots up all your mistakes and assigns a monetary value to them and then you owe him that amount of money. That's what this man from the bank does. He's a holy terror! He's a one! He comes up to you from the bank and you owe him. If you die and you have a kid then that kid owes him. This kid owes what you owed and what they owe on top of that. All to the bank. All for a few quid they do it. What of any of us survives? Our debts survive, what we owe survives. You cannot outlive that. A man used to be able to have a bath and come out clean. Now what do we have? The water that runs runs filthy and the soap is full of dogshit. It used to be that a man could take a dog out on the heath, he and the dog could run on the heath under the clouds. Now the clouds are sprinkled with chemicals so it rains permanently on the tarmacked-over heath. The dog's teeth have all been pulled out and used to make designer necklaces for the daughters of bank workers. The dog's hair has been pulled out and glued to a canvas as part of an art installation for the foyer of a bank. The dog's flesh has been filleted and fried and served with garlic croutons as a delicacy in expensive restaurants. The dog's shit has been used to make soap. The bones of the dog have been hollowed out and used to make ocarinas to be sold in new age shops. The dog's organs have been transplanted into vampire bankers to keep them alive. The dogs head has been stuffed and mounted in a trendy wine bar and given glass eyes so that it always has to be looking at the bankers sitting there and sipping their cocktails full of the sweat of workers, the blood of dogs, the sap of former trees, the soil of former meadows and thickened with crude oil and the menstrual blood of poor women. How did it used to be? It used to be that you could take a photograph of your kids, a nice photo of your own children. It used to be that you could do that! Now the banks take films every day of your kids, and you pay for them to be taken. You pay for that! The films are stored in vaults along with your kids' fingernails, bits of their hair, their bodily fluids, flakes of their skin. The bankers walk down the aisles of these vaults and laugh raucously and as they laugh coins and notes pour out of their mouths and onto the floor and the echo rings endlessly around. The banker has workers that follow him with brooms to sweep up all the money and take it to the vault where it is kept in big dirty barrels. The banker talks with a voice so high-pitched that it hurts the ears of animals. His lips are chapped and they constantly bleed crude oil which runs down his chin and drips on the floor, driving the price per barrel up and down as he chews. The banker is constantly chewing something, he constantly has something between his teeth. He usually chews twenty pound notes. His teeth are big, hard, sharp and grey. His tongue is the shape and density of a bullet. He is a one, this banker is, he truly is a one. His cheeks so sunken that he can keep wads of chewed up twenty pound notes in the hollows. His cheeks are covered in coarse stubble, hard and sharp as breadknives, which the banker uses to shred the documents of anyone trying to get their money back off him. The banker's hair is lank and long, the ends of it are dipped in the blood of anyone who ever committed suicide over a financial matter. The blood goes hard in time and the ends are snapped off to form barbs. These barbs are glued to the door handles of bank branches to stop people getting in and to the buttons of cash machines to stop people getting at their money. The banker's hair is receding at the crown; even he can do nothing to stop time. His ears are stopped up with wax. He sits and hears nothing but the rustle of notes. It is incredibly hard to get through to this banker. His eyes are black globes, they see nothing but the glint of coin. At certain times they cry tears of thick black petroleum. The tears collect in his pores and dry out his skin. His skin flakes and peels off, stained with oil. The flakes are collected together in bins and the oil is wrung out of them by minimum-wage workers in windowless rooms and used to power the buses the workers get to and from work. Gluey oil drips constantly from the banker's nose. The banker's neck is covered in tattoos of the names of countries that suffer under the bank. It used to be that a country could use a few quid to build a playground for its kids. Now all that money goes back to the bank and the bank's goons come and torch the playground and cover the burned-out swings and slides with racist graffiti. The banker's jowls hang down like big lead chicken wings. When the banker shakes these jowls it produces a bass frequency which is sympathetic to the vibrations of the human colon. This frequency causes the sphincters of people around the banker to loosen, their bowels to open. The banker then charges these people money for their shit to be picked up. Look at the banker. Just look at him. His shoulders are like big hocks of ham. Will you look at him. Will you just look at the guy. His shoulders are big and brawny but his arms are withered, they are feeble arms. They have turned a milky grey from decades of injecting a drug made up of twenty pound notes blended into a paste, petroleum, the thin jism of pubescent boys, morphine, the milk of single mothers, fragments from the mutilated genitals of torture victims, ketamine, truffle oil, expensive ice cream, dog blood, slivers of ivory, sap from cut-down rainforest trees, the tears of trafficked prostitutes etc. Despite these spindly arms, the banker's hands are massively oversized, each finger covered in rings the diameter of the wheel of a truck. The rings are made of precious metals and are encrusted with jewels stolen from the Third World. The hands constantly grope around, grasping at anything they can and stuffing it into the banker's mouth. On the banker's left hand, the nails grow in long yellow spirals; they could be miles long. The right hand, however, is perfectly manicured, the nails as smooth and sharp as art gallery walls. The banker's body is encased in a tight suit. The suit is made of trousers, a waistcoat and a jacket. The banker also wears a shirt and a tie done up real tight. He also wears socks and hard leather shoes. Not much is known about the banker's body because the suit never comes off. Take a look at the banker and think about his body. The hard, crisp lines of the suit reveal little about what is underneath. It could just be cardboard or metal. It could be meat. The banker sits at a desk and the blue glare of a computer lights up his face. The computer is a constantly updating a list of every person who ever feels unhappy, held back, constrained or despondent because of something to do with money. Anyone who is ever prevented from doing anything because of money comes up on this list. The banker's hands scratch around at the desk;

the fingernails, they are like bradawls scoring deep troughs in the wood. His eyes bore, the banker is a bore.

The bear continues to walk. The bear walks along this road. Clouds amass and roil above the hills, out in the distance past the edge of the city. At a pedestrian crossing a group of girls run into the road, crossing towards the bear. An oncoming car is forced to slow and the driver sounds the horn. The girls scream and run onto the pavement and collapse together into raucous laughter. They seem to find their collective inability to properly and safely cross a road absolutely hilarious. The bear tries to manoeuvre his way around the group, who are blocking the pavement. Some of the girls are jovially remonstrating with the first girl over her lack of forethought while she counters by admonishing them for foolishly following her and dawdling. As the bear sidesteps through the group, one girl catches his eye and her smile just drops and she jerks her face away, pulling her headscarf around it and she says something to the girl beside her, who turns, looks, and turns away again. The laughter from the group quickly gives way to whispering. The girls stand and gaze at the bear, who is now walking away from them.

The bear walks past rows of terraced houses that are hard and sharp and made of red bricks. They are shabby places. The bricks are scored by the wing mirrors of trucks and buses that pass too close, they are black with fumes, they are damp with the water that leaks from the gutters, they are green with the algae that grow on the damp brick. In one front yard two women sift listlessly through a pile of bricks and Coke cans while a toothless old man sits on the low wall. When he sees the bear he starts laughing raucously. The bear walks past another newsagent. There are side roads that go on into the distance. There are even some trees. The bear walks on. The bear walks on with the grey slabs underneath him, the houses around him, the cars that go by, the birds that line up on the telephone wires and then – wham – they all fly away at once because of the bird hivemind, the reflections in windows, the sky in the sky, the clouds, all that. The bear walks on and he encounters billions of little tiny things and, still in his suit, shoes clopping on the floor, paws swishing at his sides, eyes straight ahead, ears pricked up. The bear comes to a building site. On the far side of the site some warehouses are almost complete. They are flimsy and large buildings with thin walls arranged around a central metal structure. The big doors of one of them are open and the bear can see that all inside is black. The earth around the warehouses is all brown muck dug up by yellow diggers. The whole site is fenced in by old rusted red wrought-iron railings. The railings are all that remains of whatever the site used to be. Did it used to be a park? A housing estate? A factory? Birds circle the warehouse. Everything is relentlessly normal. The diggers drive up and down, pick up some earth, move it around. The dark mouth of the warehouse is open. Men stand around. The bear walks. A kid on a bike rides up the pavement towards the bear; his face is a hard and sad blur. He is riding right towards the bear. The bear steps to the side, closer in to the railings. The bike gains speed.

The kid's face does not move. At the last moment, as he is about to ride past, the kid swerves the bike in towards this bear, jerks the front wheel so the bike appears to be set for collision with the bear. The bear jumps with surprise because the bike is about to hit him. Then, beyond the last moment, beyond even that, the kid swerves the bike back away from the bear and all the bear feels is the rush of air as the kid and his bike go by. The bear turns and watches the kid fly along the pavement, away towards the estates and the shops and all that.

More terraced houses. The bear walks and the bear comes to a row of shops. There is also a car wash. Everything flutters in the wind. Everything sways, everything hums, everything sways. That's what everything does. It sways, it hums, it sways. The paper shop has tins of food. The carwash washes cars. The sky hangs down. It does. The birds circle. Everything sways.

The road widens and becomes a dual carriageway again. The bear walks down it. There is a McDonald's and a Blockbuster. There is, again, a shop selling the mobile phones. It has the mobile phones in the window. There is a newsagent. On the other side of the dual carriageway, fenced off, there is a park. A woman walking a dog crosses in front of the bear in the direction of the park. The dog pulls on its lead back towards the bear, showing its teeth, growling. The park is flat and has grass. The bear stands beside two recycling bins which are blue. There is a pond in the park and a playground with some swings. The bear recalls going to this park once, after a party. This is his one thought, at this time. He thinks back to that time. He rejects the thought, he rejects that thinking. He walks on, again he walks on.

The bear walks until the houses get better. They get bigger. The streets get cleaner, there is less graffiti. The people are richer, their dogs are better fed, their dogs are less vicious, their dogs are less desperate. Dogs like that, they are a different type of dog altogether. Dogs like that. Where this bear has come to, it has that reek of money. It is the suburbs of the city. Out here there is space, which the bear walks through. The sky no longer hangs, it does not. The sky is up there. The bear's walk is almost complete, don't worry.

The bear walks from the city, through the suburbs and out into the country. He is disgraced. Finally he comes to a yard full of chickens and he stops among those chickens. The chickens mill around. There is no moral dimension to the actions of chickens. As one, the chickens set upon the bear. The chickens peck at the bear's legs until he falls. The chickens peck at the bear's arms until he cannot raise them. The chickens peck until the bear is dead. They peck out his eyes, they peck at his innards. This bear that had once yearned now lies dead among chickens. The chickens consume the suit the bear wore. The chickens consume his prickly flesh. They consume his bones. There is nothing left of the bear. The chickens become poison. Anyone who eats these chickens will perish.

The crouched people and children were barely discernible from the dogs. People were mouthing words to her but their faces smeared and she could hear nothing. She pushed some sound out of her mouth. She wanted it to sound like 'No', but she couldn't tell what it sounded like. They had left the party to come to the park. Over the lip of the hill the gloaming was visible. Behind them it was still dark. Carol looked over at the group. It was cold. She could feel the drugs. Still feel them. Yeah. The drugs. Someone was saying something, but she could just hear a high-pitched whine in both ears. Someone was coming over, it was Regis, on his face a desecration of a smile. He tried to hold her steady, he put his arm around her but she pushed him away. He was saying something to her but all she could hear was this high-pitched whine in both ears. Her socks inside her shoes were getting wet in the wet grass. She turned off in another direction. She looked over at the hill. She did not know this part of town at all. Over the road she could see shops with the shutters down and two big plastic recycling bins. It wasn't clear whether the drugs were wearing off or coming on again. The others were sitting by or on the swings, swinging. She recalled leaving the party but not how they got to the park. She did not recall not being able to hear. That was something she did not recall. She fell to her knees, unable to walk any more. A couple of people came over. She recognised Regis. He was saying something but all she could hear was this high-pitched whine in both ears. He and the other person, a girl she did not recognise, tried to lift her. She allowed herself to be a dead weight, that was all she could allow. The streetlights in the town were starting to switch off as it got lighter. She could see her breath in thin, hollow streams. The girl she did not recognise was holding on to her, hugging her. Regis took most of her weight and they walked her towards the swings. Her feet dragged, her head was down, all she could see was the damp grass below her limp feet. She tried again to say a word, some words. The girl squeezed her hand. The girl walked backwards in front of her and looked into Carol's eyes. She was saying something, but because of the whine in both her ears, Carol could hear none of it. It was too much, it was all terrible. The girl was saying something to Regis and she could feel him respond but could not hear it. They reached the playground where the others were. She slumped down. All their mouths moved. Carol put her hands out onto the wet grass. It was hard to focus. It was hard to. She felt a tightness in her stomach and her mouth filled with saliva. She put her head down and was sick onto the grass. She put her hands onto the grass, on the sick, which was mostly just liquid. Her eyes were closed. Her head slumped. The pins fell out of her hair and her hair fell forward. Someone came behind her and lifted her up. She stood, supported by them, leaning back into them. Whoever was behind her grasped her shoulders. Suddenly she bolted forward, fell onto her knees and was sick again. Objects withdrew into their silent, unknowable depths. The trees receded. The high-pitched whine took on a new cadence, a more sombre tone. The dogs were just pastiches of dogs, the people just dismal outlines. Carol jammed the little finger of her right hand into her right ear. She sprawled out on all fours. From her right ear, blood ran down her cheek and dripped from her chin onto the grass. She tried to crawl. Regis put his arms around her and dragged her up. She fought against him, span and fell backwards. Her arm was in pain. She wrenched herself up and propelled herself forwards. The night was ending. She was at her coldest. Her arm was probably broken. The noise in her ears hit a new intensity that throbbed through her head, the music of disappointment. She fell again, this time the last.

Regis ran to where Carol had fallen. He turned her over. It was cold and his skin itched. He felt sober all of a sudden. There was grass and blood and sick on her dead face.

The farmer pushed his stick into the damp earth. The park wound round to a central point. There was the playground, there was the pond. Over the road the newsagent was just putting up his shutters. The farmer strode the paths, he watched the dogs. In time people would be getting up and going to work. He sat down on a bench and got out his tinfoil packet of sandwiches. Crisp packets and pieces of chip shop paper blew across the poorly grass. He threw the tinfoil onto the ground. He had nothing but contempt for the earth, the poor earth that was parcelled up into parks and streets. In the distance there was an ambulance siren. In the middle of the park a big man stood over a dead woman. The farmer prodded the soil with his stick. It was thin and loose, it was weak, it held no nourishment. He finished the sandwiches. There was nothing for him to do but get up and go.

ALSO FROM SALT